FALLOUT

DARK ROAD – BOOK FOUR

BRUNO MILLER

FALLOUT:
Dark Road, Book Four

Copyright © 2018 Bruno Miller

Find out when Bruno's next book is coming out.
Join his mailing list for release news, sales, and the occasional survival tip. No spam ever.
http://bit.ly/1kkLgHi

Published in the United States of America.

Would this be your final stand?

The journey continues for Ben, his son Joel, Joel's classmate Allie and their dog Gunner as they struggle with the harsh realities of this dangerous new world.

Forging their way past countless obstacles both natural and manmade, they slowly make their way across the country, never knowing where they will sleep, or what challenges lie ahead. But the drive to reunite with family pushes them toward the east coast.

Setbacks wait around every turn. Ben and his crew must adapt and overcome, honing their survival skills as they are repeatedly forced to fight for their lives.

Will Ben's army training get them to their loved ones in time? Or will the dark road take its toll?

THE DARK ROAD SERIES

Breakdown

Escape

Resistance

Fallout

For my kids,
for whom I'd endure anything.

· 1 ·

Ben slowly drove the truck back down the dirt road and away from the bridge.

It had been such a good night with the kids. They were all so tired last night the campsite by the river seemed to be the perfect place to rest and recover from a rough day on the road. Joel had even done a little hunting and managed to bag three ducks for dinner. Just when things seemed to be going so well for a change. This just proved to Ben that they couldn't afford to be careless and let their guard down. Now they had a serious situation to deal with, and he couldn't help but feel like it was his fault.

Ben couldn't believe he had fallen for this trap. Now they were stuck here between these two bridges by who knew what kind of people. He should have listened to his gut on the way in here. He'd known something wasn't right about those cars parked on the bridge last night.

"Do you think they heard me shooting last night?" Joel asked.

"No, they already knew we were here. They probably watched us drive in last night and shut the bridge down once we were out of sight."

Allie sighed. "I guess we should have kept going last night."

"They probably already had the bridge ahead blocked off. I'm sure they meant to catch us last night, but we probably threw them for a loop by getting off the road and spending the night a few miles downriver."

"Do you think they're looking for us?" Joel swallowed.

"I'm sure of it. We need to get this truck hidden before we do anything else." Ben sped up a little and continued down the road until they were back on the narrow, washed-out trail they had used to get to last night's campsite. He maneuvered the Blazer slowly as he leaned over the wheel and looked along the side of the trail for any kind of opening or break in the vegetation.

After a few minutes they reached an area where the trees thinned out a little into dense brush. Ben spotted a small break in the undergrowth, turned off the trail, and went into the woods.

Still in four-wheel drive from yesterday, the Chevy clawed its way up over the dense vegetation. The branches fought back and scratched at the sides and bottom of the truck but were no match for the machine.

Once over the initial brush along the edge of the trail, the woods opened up, leaving plenty of room between the mature trees to navigate. They went about a mile or so before the semisolid ground under the truck turned to swampy lowlands. Ben was forced to stop for fear of getting stuck.

He found a thick area of tall marsh grass and phragmites that would make a good place to conceal the truck. As he eased the Blazer into the thicket, he felt the wet ground give way. He was careful to only go as far as they needed to get the truck covered past the tailgate a couple feet.

"We can use the camo netting to finish the job." Ben shut the truck off and eased out, pushing the marsh grass aside with the door as he opened it.

"Watch your step. It's a little muddy out here." Joel looked back at Allie as he got out. Gunner appeared totally confused by the unexpected stop and hesitantly followed Allie out of the truck.

Ben opened the back of the truck and started organizing gear on the tailgate. He found the large piece of camo netting folded up and dragged it out.

He handed it to Joel. "How about you guys start covering the truck?"

"Got it." Joel took the netting and pushed his way through the grass to the hood of the truck.

Allie followed behind, being careful not to get whipped with the tall grass as she tried to stay in the freshly made path behind Joel.

They each took a side at the front of the Blazer and spread the netting out lengthwise before they unfolded it over the truck. They worked their way back, climbing up on the tires so they could get it over the rooftop cargo box. Stopping at the rear of the cab, they left the remainder piled up on the roof.

By the time Joel and Allie had the truck mostly covered, Ben had an assortment of weapons and gear laid out across the tailgate.

"Here you go. Take these and get out of this mud." Ben handed Joel the already-loaded AR-15 and a few extra magazines.

Joel stuffed the extra mags in his rear pockets and took the rifle from his dad, slinging it over his shoulder.

Then Ben handed Allie the modified Weatherby shotgun along with a handful of shells. "It's already loaded and ready to go. Safety's on."

"Thanks." She divided the shells up and filled her front jean pockets, pushing four shotgun shells into each one.

"We need to find a good vantage point where you guys can be a safe distance away from the truck but close enough to keep an eye on it." Ben stopped what he was doing long enough to quickly scan their surroundings. "Maybe somewhere over there?" He nodded toward an area of higher ground before turning his attention back to what he was doing.

Joel wrinkled his brow. "We're not going with you?"

"No. It's better if I go alone. I just need to do a little recon and see if I can find out what and who we're dealing with here. Besides, I need you guys to watch the truck." Ben continued to load his M24 without looking up.

"What if you need help?" Joel asked. It was clear the kid wanted to come.

"I need you to stay here to keep an eye on things. I'll be fine." Ben looked at Joel this time and made eye contact in an effort to end the debate.

Joel accepted his father's decision and joined Allie several feet back from the truck on higher ground, out of the mud and marsh grass.

Gunner, already unnecessarily coated in the thick brown muck they had parked in, followed Joel. He seemed pleased with the mess he had become and lazily sat down near where Allie was standing.

"Ugh…you're such a piglet!" Joel looked at Gunner, who seemed to ignore the comment.

Allie scratched Gunner's head. "Awe, he's a good boy."

Ben tossed the hatchet up onto the dry ground a few feet away from the kids. "Why don't you guys start looking for a spot to hide?" He hated to leave them here on their own, but he wanted to move fast and move quiet—something he could do better alone. Plus, they could keep in touch using the two-way radios if necessary.

By his estimate, only a couple miles separated them from the bridge out of Missouri, and he could get back to the kids in a hurry if he had to. What other choice did he have but to leave the kids there? He had already put them in enough danger by letting his guard down again and getting them into a bad situation. He resolved to stop beating himself up over it. There would be plenty of time for that later. Right now, he had to focus on what needed to be done.

· 2 ·

Joel picked up the small hatchet. He knew immediately that his dad wanted him to make a blind for him and Allie to hide in. He had made plenty before on their hunting trips, but this time would be different.

This time they were the ones being hunted.

Joel wished he could go with his dad and wanted to help him, but it slowly dawned on him that maybe the real reason his dad wanted him to stay behind was to keep an eye on Allie. After what had happened to her at the gas station back in Kansas, he was happy not to let her out of his sight for a while.

Joel was suddenly reminded by the harsh reality that he had killed a man just a couple days ago. Not that he needed to be reminded of that. It was something he would never forget. He could still see the man's dirty face as he pulled the trigger. The scene played out in his mind over and over in slow motion.

He knew he'd had no choice. It had been an "us or them" situation, like his dad would say, but that didn't make what he had done any easier to swallow. No matter how many times he told himself he was justified in pulling that trigger, he still felt a sense of guilt about taking a life. He was glad most of the confrontation had gone a little blurry in his mind. He remembered more details than he wanted to already.

Allie followed Joel to an old, dead fallen tree.

"This looks like a good spot," Joel said.

Allie studied the tree, which had been uprooted and toppled over. The mature oak was a significant size and stretched along the ground, all the way down into the marshy area near where they had concealed the Blazer in the tall grass. The trunk was only about 40 yards away from the truck, but the way the tree had fallen, with its large root ball still intact, would provide them exceptional cover if anyone approached from the trail.

Joel looked down the gradual slope to where his dad was closing up the truck and pulling the camo netting the rest of the way over the back of the Blazer. Between the flat tan paint job, blackened windows, and camouflage netting, the Blazer had become invisible.

His dad straightened the marsh grass where it had been pushed aside from their activity, then walked away from the truck, his bag and rifle slung over his shoulder. He joined Joel and Allie up on the high ground out of the marsh.

"What do you think about behind that tree? I can fill in underneath with some brush." Joel pointed along the ground to where the tree fell short of connecting with the dirt by several inches.

"Yeah, that'll work." Ben handed one of the two-way radios to Joel. "Keep the volume low and don't use it unless you have to. If you can't talk, give me two short clicks. If I hear that, I'll know you've got trouble and I'll double-time it back here."

Joel nodded. "Okay."

Ben looked at both of them. "You both have your pistols, right?"

"Yes," Joel answered quickly.

"Yep." Allie reached down to her hip and touched her hand to the holstered .38. "Is Gunner staying with us?"

"Yeah. I think it's a good idea. He knows how to be quiet in a blind and he'll be able to hear anybody coming long before you guys will," Ben said.

"Be careful, Dad," Joel said.

"I will. I'll be back as soon as I can." And with that, Ben headed off into the woods.

Joel turned to look at Allie as she stood there in her mud-encrusted hiking boots, holding the shotgun in one hand with the other resting on the .38.

She was a different person than the girl he had found hiding in the attic less than a week ago. She was somehow stronger in spite of the circumstances. For all they had been through, she gave off a confidence that was contagious. She somehow made him feel like there was hope and a reason to believe everything would be okay again someday.

Or maybe it was the fact he was falling hopelessly in love with her.

· 3 ·

Ben hated leaving them there but he'd make better time on his own. As soon as he could figure out what was going on, he'd get back to the kids, and they could come up with a plan.

He headed east toward the bridge, jogging when the vegetation allowed. The peninsula they were on was only a few miles wide according to the map. He wished the atlas was more detailed, but he was fortunate to at least have what he did.

He tried to cut an angle through the woods that would take him close to the main road. The ground would be higher and easy to navigate. On the map, this area looked pretty wet, and he didn't want to get stuck wading through any marshy areas.

Also, if he kept to the woods, just off the road, he could watch for any patrolling vehicles, although if their trappers had been looking for them since last night, they may have resorted to searching the woods as well by now.

He was glad he had listened to his instincts last night and gotten them well off the road. He wondered if the kids thought he was being too cautious by going so far past the end of the trail. He hadn't wanted to mention his suspicions at the time and cause them to worry for no reason.

Of course, none of that mattered now.

He was going to have to remind himself to be honest with Joel and Allie and not hold back with any information or observations he made. They needed to be part of the decision-making process from now on, and they deserved it. They were both holding up well, all things considered. He knew the journey would be hard but he hadn't realized it would get this bad this quickly. He was not only impressed, but also proud of them.

Joel had really stepped up his game, and Ben had noticed a big change in him. And even though he hadn't known Allie for very long, he found himself thinking of her like one of his own kids. He was equally impressed with how she had handled herself up to this point.

Considering the loss of her mother and the uncertainty of her father's well-being, Ben thought she was a real trooper. After all the stuff they'd seen and been through in the last few days, he doubted there were many kids their age that could keep their composure as well as they had.

They'd had such a good travel day yesterday it was hard to accept the fact that things had deteriorated into the situation they were in now. He wouldn't be able to live with himself if anything happened to Joel or Allie.

When Ben thought about how much time this was costing them and the potential danger they might be in, anger wormed up his spine. He resented whoever was behind it. In his opinion, there was nothing worse than a person who was willing to harm others for personal gain.

He'd seen the strong take advantage of the weak too many times in some of the places he'd been stationed over the years. He'd seen the suffering and the hardship firsthand. In part, that was what convinced him terminate his Army career. Nothing ever changed in these places they were sent to. Wiping out one faction only created a void for a new and sometimes far more nefarious version to step in. Oftentimes the locals were left no better off than they had been at the start.

Ben focused on the way in front of him. He could make out an area ahead where the tree canopy thinned out considerably. He altered his course to run alongside the clearing. Glimpses of the road were visible through the thinning vegetation.

He maintained a somewhat steady pace now in the sparse woods and was only limited by his own aches and pains. This was the farthest he had run in a few years and the first time he had felt his age in a while.

A few more minutes in, he stopped and rested the rifle against a tree while he wriggled out of the backpack and took off his long-sleeve overshirt. He balled it up and stuffed it in the backpack as he glanced at his surroundings from time to time.

With a sigh, he repositioned the pack and caught his breath. Picking the M24 back up, he stood motionless for a minute or two and listened. He didn't hear any cars, and he hadn't seen anything yet.

Maybe whoever was doing this to them had given up looking and was now waiting at a roadblock ahead. If that was the case, it would make things simple. He wouldn't have to worry about the kids or the truck.

Of course, he'd have no way of knowing how many they were up against, but all that really mattered was getting across that bridge. It wasn't his responsibility to make it safe for any other travelers that might come after them.

If he was ever going to see Bradley and Emma again, he had to be selfish. At least that's what he told himself. Too bad his conscience wasn't buying it.

· 4 ·

Ben could see open sky past the trees a few hundred yards ahead. He slowed to a brisk walk while he got his bearings.

On the map, Route 67 cut across the peninsula in a broad arc that curved right. He had been following the curve of the road for a while now, and he must have been close to where the bridge started. The map also showed a thin strip of land that ran under the bridge for a bit before stopping at the river. But he would see for himself soon enough.

He slowly picked his way through the last several feet of underbrush until the bridge came into view. He crouched alongside a large tree at the edge of the clearing. Once positioned, he slid off the strap of the rifle sling and brought it around to his shoulder. He flipped the lens covers up and surveyed the bridge through the 10 × 42 scope.

It was much larger than the first bridge they crossed last night but still had only two lanes on each side. The concrete median that separated the east- and westbound traffic was much wider. In the middle of the bridge were two concrete pillars that must have been 100 feet tall. Long, round steel supports ran from the top of the columns and down the bridge, forming two giant inverted steel cones. It was impressive to say the least, but all Ben was interested in was looking for blockages.

He turned the ring on the scope up to 10, taking full advantage of the magnification it offered. He scanned the bridge, starting from the far side and looking for any roadblocks, accidental or otherwise. Unable to believe his eyes, he had to scan the bridge again from one end to the other.

It was clear, at least what he could see of it from here. This should have given him some measure of relief but it didn't. It was too good to be true, and he knew it. Outside of a busy town the size of Alton, there should have been at least a car or two on the bridge.

A few hundred yards of dense woods remained between Ben and the start of the bridge. The four-lane bridge ran into the tree line he was using for cover. The woods prevented him from seeing exactly where the highway funneled onto the bridge. He was going to have to get closer to inspect the rest of it.

He closed up the scope and slung the rifle over his shoulder. He was careful to hike through the woods much more slowly now as he approached the edge of the road. Taking his time to go around vegetation and dry leaves when he would rather go through them, he was trying to make as little noise as possible.

As he got closer he started to make out the shapes of vehicles on the road at the beginning of the bridge. He crept to a nearby tree and took a knee. With a hand on the tree, he used his arm for a gun rest and looked through the scope at the massive mountain of mangled cars and trucks that walled off the entrance to the bridge.

They were piled two or three vehicles high and as many as two or three deep in some parts of the makeshift roadblock. No one was coming or going over this bridge. Clearly, this was meant to isolate this side from Alton on a permanent basis for whatever reason.

Whoever had done this must have had access to some large equipment, like what Ben had seen back at the quarry they passed yesterday.

Ben's mind began to work as he started to piece together what little information he had. Immediately, he wondered if there was some connection there. But more importantly, how were they going to get around this?

They would have to go north to get to the next bridge across the Mississippi, and he knew that was realistically a day's travel away. There was no guarantee the next bridge would be open, either. All these river crossings would be choke points where people could be funneled through and exploited by those who chose to do so.

Just like this one.

At the sound of a vehicle coming down the road, Ben instinctively dropped to the prone position. He pulled the rifle in close to his body as he scooted alongside an old log and watched.

A blue Ford Bronco drove by. Its big mud tires whirred as they rolled over the pavement at high speed. It looked like there was only a driver in the truck.

He got within 20 yards of the roadblock and stopped in the center of the road. The driver shut the engine off and got out. The man wore a red ball cap and carried some type of hunting rifle as he walked to the edge of the highway and stood there like he was waiting on someone.

A brown Chevy pickup emerged from the opposite side of the woods and drove onto the shoulder, where the man was waiting. The Chevy parked and two men got out and walked to the man in the ball cap. They both carried guns as well. The passenger had a shotgun and the driver had a large-caliber pistol that he stuffed into his belt behind his back as he approached the other guy.

"Any luck?" the man with the shotgun asked.

"Nothing," the man in the ball cap replied. "But I'll tell you this: they said not to come back to the quarry until we found them."

Ben strained to hear what the men were talking about.

"Man, that's bull! We've been out here all night. It's not like they're going anywhere!" The driver of the pickup threw his hands in the air as he turned to look at the pile of cars blocking the bridge.

"I'm just tellin' ya what they said to me on the radio. Talk to 'em yourself if you want." The man in the ball cap offered him what looked like a handheld radio.

"Forget it. They don't care about us." The pickup driver waved him off and pulled out a pack of cigarettes instead. He lit one up as he leaned against the hood of the truck.

"They oughta turn up soon. It's still early," the man with the shotgun said.

"Well, I guess I'm gonna check downriver a little ways from the other bridge again. That's the last place we saw them last night. They gotta be around there somewhere. Maybe I'll go all the way down to that old trail this time. Why don't one of you come with me?" the man in the red ball cap asked.

The man with the shotgun stepped forward immediately. "I'll go."

"Oh, come on, man!" The guy smoking stood up straight. "I always get stuck here while you guys have all the fun," he hollered.

"Somebody's gotta stay here in case they come this way. Besides, you're a lousy shot." The man in the ball cap pulled out a can of dip. "I had to finish the last guy off for you."

A chill ran through Ben's veins when he heard that, and he immediately understood what type of lowlifes he was dealing with.

"You try shooting at a moving car and do better." The man took a long draw off the cigarette, then threw it on the ground before heading around to the back of the pickup. He reached into the truck bed, pulled out a beer, and cracked it open. "Just go find them so we can go back. I'm starvin' out here," he whined before taking a long drink from the can.

"All right then." The Bronco driver loaded his lip. "Stay alert and quit screwin' around." He spat on the ground before heading for his truck.

The man with the shotgun scurried around to the other side and jumped in. They turned around while the other guy stayed by his truck and leaned over the bed as he drank his beer.

The driver leaned out his window and said something before they drove off, but Ben couldn't hear him over the truck's exhaust.

At least he knew how many people they were dealing with. He felt it was safe to assume it was just the three of them at this point, although by the sounds of it, there were more members of the group back at the quarry.

He could worry about the others later. Right now, he had to deal with these three — and quickly.

Two of them were headed straight for Joel and Allie.

· 5 ·

It all made sense to Ben now. From the quarry, they could see any travelers headed east as they passed by. Then they could swoop in behind them, closing off the first bridge and any chance of escape.

By the time the unsuspecting victims realized the second bridge was blocked, it would be too late. If they tried to make a run for it, they would soon realize they were trapped in the middle.

All three of those guys had probably been waiting at the second bridge for them last night. It was a good thing they had gotten off the road and not gone any farther.

Ben and the kids would have had to face all three at once, and he didn't like those odds. While he had confidence in Joel's ability to handle himself with a gun, he knew neither Joel nor especially Allie was prepared for a shootout.

Ben had no choice but to take these guys out. At this point, he couldn't assume anything but the worst about their captors and their intentions for him and the kids. These men were armed and dangerous killers—and it was time to deal with them.

He waited until the blue Bronco was out of sight. He hoped the other two men wouldn't hear the shot from his .338 Lapua, but just in case, he'd stay put for a minute or two and be ready for them if they came back his way.

He had a good vantage point over the road from his position, and he could easily take out the driver before the two even made it back to check on their friend. While he waited, he could reach out to Joel on the radio and warn him.

Through his scope, Ben watched the man drink his beer. As the crosshairs drifted across the man's head, Ben squeezed the trigger smoothly… *BANG!* The gun jerked back and up for a split-second, and when the scope came down again, the man was no longer in the crosshairs. Only a large bloody splatter—and a bullet hole—remained on the side of the truck bed.

Ben glanced at the body to confirm the man was dead. The only movement came from the half-empty beer can rolling around on the ground and leaving a trail as it spilled its contents.

Ben was satisfied the job was done but unhappy he had to do it. It was an emotion he hadn't felt in a long time and one he'd hoped to leave behind when he parted ways with the Army.

Ben quickly shifted his position to face down the road while he dug through the backpack and grabbed the radio.

"Joel, come in. It's Dad. Over."

"I'm here. Go ahead. Over."

"There are two guys with guns headed down the trail we were on. One scoped rifle and one shotgun. Stay put. On my way to you. Over."

"Copy that."

"I repeat: stay put. Watch your 12 o'clock. Start radio silence. Over"

"Roger that. Over"

Ben listened to see if he could hear the Bronco coming back. Maybe they hadn't heard the shot after all. The exhaust had been kind of loud, but he really wished they had picked up on it now.

He was going to have to beat them to the kids.

Rather than run back through the woods, he decided to make use of the beer drinker's pickup. He threw his bag over his shoulder and grabbed his gun, securing both things. He pushed up off the ground and sprinted for the old Chevy.

All he could think about was how he hoped the dead guy had left the keys in the ignition. When he got to the truck, he did his best to ignore the chunks of gray matter splattered across the bed rail. Some of the blood was already beginning to dry on the truck's side in the hot morning sun.

"Yes." Ben sighed with relief as he reached over the steering column and felt the keys hanging in the ignition.

He threw his bag in and laid his rifle across the far side of the bench seat. Then he hesitated, but after a second of thought, he decided to drag the body off the road and into the bushes. Always a good idea to cover his tracks when possible. Unfortunately, there was nothing he could do about the large pool of blood in the road and the trail he had made by dragging the body.

Satisfied the body was sufficiently hidden, he scrambled back, got in the truck, and fired it up. It was a manual transmission with a stick on the floor.

"Been a while since I've driven one of these," he said to himself. His Jeep back in Durango was an automatic. The last time he drove something with a manual transmission was in high school, when he had his old Toyota pickup truck. Overcompensating with the gas pedal, he spun the rear tires on the blacktop as the truck lurched forward. He grabbed the shifter, and after grinding his way up through the gears, he was speeding down the road in no time. The old Chevy needed a new clutch badly, but it sure beat running.

If he couldn't catch them on the road, he would have to get as close as he could and cut through the woods the rest of the way on foot and try to head them off. Either way, the truck would save him time and energy. And he didn't have to be careful with it, because it wasn't his.

At least Joel and Allie were hidden well and the Blazer was camouflaged. If these two guys got lucky and managed to follow the kids' trail, at least they had that big tree to hide behind and use for cover. If they had to fight, they would have an easily defendable position.

The men would be approaching the kids head-on, so Joel and Allie would have the upper hand. Fortunately, Ben doubted these two idiots would be able to find Joel and Allie, at least not right away. After all, they stayed hidden all night by taking only a few common-sense precautions.

As Ben rounded the long curve in the road, the first bridge and the turnoff to the dirt road came into view. He mashed down on the gas pedal, trying to cover the last mile as quickly as possible. The Bronco was nowhere to be seen. They must have already been on the dirt road, along the river.

They would have to slow down or risk tearing their truck apart on the crater-filled trail. That was where he would make up time. Not caring about this old pickup meant he could push it to the limit on the trail. This truck was a onetime use for him and he'd rather not leave these lowlifes a working vehicle anyways.

Ben hardly slowed as he hit the turnoff before the bridge. The rear end of the pickup fishtailed on the loose gravel, spitting rocks into the air. He quickly downshifted and hit the gas, forcing the truck to straighten out.

The dirt road that ran along the river was just up ahead. The bright mid-morning sun reflected off a lingering dust cloud that hung over the intersection.

It was the first sign he was gaining on the men in the Ford Bronco.

· 6 ·

Now Ben wondered if he should confront the men on the road or follow them from a distance. He'd have the element of surprise either way. The guys in the Bronco would think it was their friend chasing them down for something. They obviously hadn't left him with a radio.

Ben had hoped to find one in the truck when he'd commandeered it, but he hadn't seen a radio in here anywhere or on the driver.

He slowed as he approached and slid the last couple of feet into the gravel intersection before stopping. He could see a good distance down the dirt road to his left, but still no Bronco. How were they so far ahead?

The road followed the contours of the river so he could see only a few hundred yards before it veered off to the right and out of sight. He spun the tires as he turned the wheel to the left and continued his pursuit.

After a few minutes of hard driving, he expected to see the Ford around the next bend any minute now, but he didn't. They must have been going pretty fast.

He pushed the old Chevy even harder as it rattled down the pothole-laden road. He was definitely getting closer. The dusty trail the Bronco had left in its wake was starting to come in the windows and fill the cabin in the pickup. Ben paid it no mind and sped up even more, grimacing as the truck shook violently and skated over a washboard section of road.

Then, as he was coming around a sharp corner, he caught a glimpse of a red tail light as it disappeared around some thick bushes ahead. They were nearing the end of the dirt road and would soon be on the narrow trail that led to last night's campsite.

But more importantly, it would take them past the kids. He couldn't risk them finding the trail they'd made with the Blazer and didn't plan on letting them get that far. It would only take a matter of minutes to find the trail the kids forged through the woods.

Time to make a move.

Ben let the Bronco turn onto the trail before he gunned the pickup and pulled in behind them.

When he'd first got in the pickup back at the roadblock, he noticed a camo ball cap on the seat. He grabbed it now and put it on. The hat might buy him a few extra seconds of disguise if they thought he was the other guy.

Ben blew the horn and slammed on the brakes simultaneously. He stopped the pickup and pushed the long stick shifter forward until it slipped out of gear while he waited for their reaction. A few seconds went by without a response, and he was just about to blow the horn again when he saw the red glow from the Bronco's brake lights.

"Here we go," he muttered. He opened his door and got ready as he pulled the Glock out of his concealed holster from the small of his back. With one foot out of the truck and the other still on the brake, Ben positioned himself in the opening between the door and the truck.

With his gun at the ready, he waited. The driver's door swung open as the man put it in park and got out.

"What do you want now? Hey—"

But it was too late; Ben had already lined up the shot. *BANG! BANG!*

The driver, two shots to his chest, went down where he stood. Ben turned his attention to the passenger, who was only halfway out of the Bronco by now.

"Hey...hey, who are you?" The passenger raised his shotgun as he came around the back of the Bronco, but he was too slow.

BANG! Ben shot him once in the chest.

He staggered a couple steps back and dropped the shotgun. He clutched his chest and fell on the ground. "You…you sh-shot me."

Ben walked over to where the man had fallen, keeping one eye on the driver as best he could to make sure there was no movement. Two shots center mass should have killed him, but he wasn't taking any chances without any backup.

"How many more at the quarry?" Ben trained the Glock on the man's head.

The man was bleeding badly. Ben didn't have much time to get information out of him. He lay there with his right hand covering the wound but failed to stop the blood gushing out and through his fingers. His left hand trembled as he wiped sweat off his forehead, leaving a bloody trail.

"T-t-two more," he sputtered. "Hel-help m…" His eyes rolled back into his head and his body went limp before he could get the words out.

Ben took a few steps back and headed over to the driver. He was face-down in the dirt and gave no response when Ben used his foot to push one of his arms away from his torso.

He jogged back to the pickup and got the radio out of his bag.

"Joel, come in. Over"

"Go ahead, Dad. Over."

"The gunshots were me. I took care of the guys headed your way. Stay put. I'm coming to you. Over."

"Roger that. Staying put. Over."

But first, Ben needed to clear the narrow trail of the vehicles so they could get back out this way. He ran to the pickup and grabbed his gun and pack out of the cab. Setting them on the ground a few feet away, he returned to the pickup.

He leaned into the cab and turned the wheel to the right, then put it in gear and popped the clutch.

The old Chevy shot forward as Ben jumped clear, leaving the driver's side door open. The truck drove itself over the edge of the trail, where it forced its way through the undergrowth before hitting a tree. The rear tires continued to spin in vain as the engine sputtered and finally stalled.

Ben decided to get the bodies off the road. He wasn't worried about covering his trail here, but there was no reason to leave them on display for the kids to see. And they were going to have to come through here on their way back to the main road.

Then do what? He hadn't planned that far ahead yet, although he had a few ideas.

Without a large piece of equipment, there was no way of clearing that bridge. Even as it stood, it was going to take considerable effort to clear the smaller bridge just to get back across to where they had come from. If they drove up to the next closest crossing, it would be a day's drive at least. And an alternate route could add even more time to the overall trip by taking them too far north.

Ben glanced at his watch. By the time they got the bridge cleared, it would be pushing noon. They wouldn't even make the next bridge today and would have to camp yet again on the west side of the Mississippi. The thought of that sounded too much like defeat to Ben.

They had to do better. Solving the situation here was starting to make a lot of sense. They would have to deal with the remaining bad guys, but if there were only two of them left, it shouldn't be a problem.

If they could get their hands on one of those front-end loaders from the quarry, they could make quick work of the big roadblock in no time. He was pretty sure that's what the men had used to pile the cars up in the first place.

He'd have to work out the details in his head and run it all past Joel and Allie. He'd need their help on this one. Hopefully the guy was telling the truth about there only being two others. Ben wasn't sure how much he was willing to gamble on a dead man's words.

· 7 ·

Ben took a look inside the Bronco before getting in. It was still running and both doors were open. The two-way radio was on the floor between the seats but was turned off. On the back seat sat a box of shotgun shells and a soft rifle case that Ben presumed had the driver's gun inside and maybe some ammo in the pocket.

Otherwise, the truck was empty, except for a few empty dip cans on the floor along with some other trash. He put his gun and bag on the passenger's seat before leaning all the way over and pulling the opposite door closed. He got settled into the driver's seat and closed the door.

"Come in, Joel. Over."

"Go ahead. Over"

"I'll be in a blue Ford Bronco coming in on the trail we made. Over."

"Okay. I mean copy that. Over."

Ben put the Bronco in gear and continued down the trail. The truck seemed like it was in good shape. Someone had taken care of it, unlike the pickup he'd borrowed. He figured the Ford would get back into the woods to where the Blazer was stashed without any trouble.

The more he thought about it, the more he realized the Bronco might actually be the key to getting out of this mess. He could disguise himself in the Bronco and catch the others over at the quarry off guard. They wouldn't suspect anything if they saw a familiar vehicle coming. At least he hoped it would fool them.

The people at the quarry would probably be expecting one of the guys to return sooner or later. From what he'd heard of their conversation back at the roadblock, it sounded like the men had been searching for him and the kids between the bridges for a while.

There was one problem with the plan that stood out. From the quarry, the remaining men had a good view of the smaller bridge and would be able to see anyone coming. Ben and his crew were going to have to stop at mid-span and push the cars out of the way.

If the people over at the quarry were paying attention, they'd spot him and the kids. The last thing Ben wanted was for them to get in a gunfight on the middle of the bridge while trying to move the cars. But pushing the cars out of the way would take all three of them, and they would be exposed the whole time.

Right now, he couldn't think of any other options. As much as he didn't like the plan, he knew they needed one of those big loaders from the quarry to move the tangled mess of cars from the other bridge. He wasn't sure how else to go about getting one without being seen.

When they'd driven by the quarry yesterday, he'd noticed a small remote building set back from the front office entrance. There were several pieces of heavy equipment parked around it, and Ben suspected they would find keys to one of the loaders in there.

He had driven an articulated loader in the army once, when they had gotten roped into helping set up a forward operating base. The FOB was supposed to be operational when they got there, but that was far from the case due to heavy hostile activity. He spent a few hours on the hulking piece of equipment, and by the end, he was actually having a good time running it.

For its size, the six-ton loader was easy to operate and the controls were pretty intuitive. There were only a couple pedals on the floor, and it was a simple forward or reverse selector on the column. If Joel and Allie could get one running, he could deal with the remaining bad guys.

The quarry's front office looked like it had originally been a house and maybe still was. The house sat up on a hill at the front of the property, just off the highway and about 50 yards or so inside the fence. The whole place was surrounded by chain link fence with barbed wire at the top.

The only entrance he'd seen was up front by the house, and as he recalled, the gate was shut when they'd driven by yesterday. The house had a commanding view of the quarry yard, the highway, and the bridge. Most likely, that's where these guys were operating.

Ben glanced at the keys dangling from the ignition. There was a smaller brass key on the ring that looked like it could belong to a padlock. Maybe that opened the gate. Of course, getting out to open the gate or plowing through it with the Bronco would give them away just the same. The longer he thought the plan through, the more flaws he found with it.

Ben leaned his head back and spotted the trail leading into the woods from the Blazer on the left-hand side. He'd make sure he covered their tracks a little better next time they had to hide the truck.

Ben squeezed the call button on his radio as he used his other hand to guide the truck into the bushes. "Coming down the trail now. Over."

"Copy that. Over."

Ben maneuvered the Bronco along the same route they had forged with the Blazer earlier this morning. It didn't take long before the tall marsh grass and the fallen tree where Joel and Allie were hiding came into view. He pulled over close to where the Blazer was hidden and shut off the engine.

Gunner ran around from behind the tree with his hackles up as he eyed the strange vehicle warily. When Ben opened the door and got out, Gunner let his guard down. His mood change was visible as his tail whipped back and forth and he ran to Ben, playfully howling at him.

"Hey, boy, it's me. It's okay." Ben gave Gunner a few rough scratches around his neck before the dog moved on to sniff the Ford and explore it for himself.

Joel and Allie emerged from their makeshift blind behind the dead tree and walked toward Ben.

"Well, what happened?" Joel asked.

"The bridge is blocked, and I don't mean a few cars pushed across the lanes. I mean blocked as in 10–15 cars piled up. Three guys showed up, and I overheard a lot of what they said. Apparently, they're based out of the quarry across the river, and we're not the first ones they've trapped here. I took care of the guys and they were the only ones here as far as I know. There are two more of them at the quarry."

"Are you okay?" Allie looked at his hands. They were a little blood-stained from moving the bodies.

Ben looked down. "Um...yeah. I'm good. It's not mine." He hadn't realized he'd gotten blood on them. He dashed to the edge of the marsh and crouched to wash them in the muddy water. He used some of the mud to scrub the stains off.

"We're going to need a big piece of equipment to move those cars." Ben tried to shift the focus onto something else.

"Like something from the quarry?" Joel's eyes widened.

Ben nodded as he washed. "One of those big loaders would do it."

"What about going another way? Like going to another bridge somewhere?" Allie asked.

"That was the first thing I thought of, but we're talking about a day, at the minimum. The way things have been going, probably two. I don't know if your dad or the kids have that kind of time." The words came out of Ben's mouth before he could stop himself. There was an awkward silence for a few moments.

It was the truth, and he had to be honest with them. Ben stood and dried his hands on his pants as he faced the kids. "I'm sorry. But that's the way it is. I'm not going to lie to you guys or try to sell it any other way. You deserve better than that."

"Thanks Dad. It's okay. We know." Joel nodded.

"Yeah, thanks for being honest, Mr. Davis, and not treating us like kids. We can handle it. I promise." Allie managed a smile, but Ben was still worried he had said too much.

He knew they had to hear it, but it didn't make it any easier to swallow. He had better get used to it, though, because he had a feeling the worst was yet to come.

· 8 ·

Joel and Allie stood alongside the Bronco, and Allie strained on her tiptoes to see through the back window.

"There's something back here. It looks like a box or something," she said. The windows were so dirty it was a wonder she could see anything at all.

"Here you go." Ben tossed the Ford keys to Joel. "Take a look in the back. I need to get some water and a Clif bar or something before I do anything else." Ben headed for the Blazer. He pushed into the grass a few feet and rolled the camo netting over the rear of the truck so he could access the gear in the back. He quickly found a water bottle and a Clif bar.

Food in hand, he sat down on the tailgate and began going over things in his head.

"Hey, Dad, you might want to come look at this," Joel suggested.

"Coming." Ben sighed and took a gulp of the tepid water as he got off the tailgate and headed toward them. *Now what?* He walked around the back of the Bronco, where both kids were staring wide-eyed at something.

"What is it?" Ben asked as he came around the side of the truck and saw for himself.

"Is that what I think it is?" Joel asked.

"Unless there's something else in that box," Ben answered. "That looks like dynamite."

There, in the back of the Bronco, was a wooden crate that read "DANGER/EXPLOSIVES" in red letters and several languages. The words Dyno Nobel / Unimax were stenciled on the lid. There was also a small diamond-shaped chemical sign with 1.1D/1 stamped on it, indicating explosives.

Ben knew very little about dynamite, other than why the army didn't use it. Dynamite was an NG (nitroglycerine)-based explosive and was therefore not used in combat operations. NG explosives were shock-sensitive, meaning they could go off if they took a hit from a bullet or grenade fragment.

Ben eased the box onto the tailgate and slowly removed the top of the wooden crate.

Inside, the crate was almost full to the top with neatly stacked yellow tubes. Each one was about eight inches long and an inch or bigger around. A short roll of fuse cord was also coiled up inside the box. Small black writing on each stick indicated they were eight ounces in size and an 80-percent mix.

These were the real deal. Ben realized each tube was a *full* stick of dynamite. He did the math in his head twice to make sure he was coming up with the right number.

"You're looking at roughly 40 pounds of dynamite." Ben stood back for a minute and put his hand on his chin. A whole new world of possibilities had just opened up to them. This was definitely a game-changer.

"Is it dangerous?" Allie asked.

"It should be all right. Depends on how old it is. It can destabilize over time. The old stuff used to, at least. I'm not sure about this stuff." Ben picked up one of the yellow sticks and inspected it. The manufactured date was stamped on the bottom. The dynamite was less than a year old.

"It's not very old. It should be pretty safe. I still wouldn't go riding around with it in the back of my truck like these guys were," Ben added.

"What are they doing with dynamite anyway?" Joel asked.

"They must use it at the quarry for blasting rock." Ben shrugged and sat on the tailgate next to the wooden crate. It felt good to sit down. His recon mission turned assault had drained his energy and he needed a break, at least a few minutes to finish the Clif bar and rehydrate.

Ben glanced at Joel. "How about pulling the netting off the Blazer and getting it ready to go? I don't want to stay here any longer than we have to."

"Okay. No problem." Joel nodded and looked at Allie. "Want to give me a hand with the net?"

"Sure." Allie smiled. "Want me to get you anything, Mr. Davis."

"No, thanks." Ben shook his head, then took a bite of the bar.

The kids headed for the Blazer.

He sat for a few minutes while they got the truck squared away. He was starting to have some other ideas about how to deal with their situation. His first thought, when they found the dynamite, was to blast the cars out of the way at the big roadblock and not worry about the quarry or the loader.

But his real concern with that plan was the potential to damage the bridge. What good would it do to blow the cars out of the way if they destroyed the bridge in the process? He was still tempted to give it a try, though, mostly because he wasn't excited in the least over the prospects of breaking into the quarry and taking a loader. There could be a dozen bad guys over there for all he knew. And even if there were only two others, they would still have the advantage over him and the kids. The Bronco would only disguise them for so long.

The quarry might be attempting to contact their guys over here at this very moment. With that in mind, Ben got up and went to get the two-way radio off the floor in the Bronco. Joel and Allie were packing the camo netting in the back of the Blazer already. They would be able to move soon.

He turned the radio on as he walked back to his seat on the tailgate. Without an answer, the people at the quarry would grow suspicious and eventually end up coming over here to see what was going on for themselves.

Then it dawned on Ben. Maybe he wanted them to come to over.

In fact, he could take it one step further and lure them to this side of the river rather than wait around for them to act.

Ben tried to think of a way he could create a sense of urgency, or something that would force their hand into action. But he also didn't want to tip them off that he and the kids were wise to them.

The bad guys would have to use one of the loaders to clear the first roadblock and get over here. There was a good chance they would also bring another vehicle and leave the loader on the bridge when they were done moving the cars. That was fine with him if it worked out that way. No need to risk a fight on their turf when they could get these idiots to practically deliver a loader for them.

Ben heard the Blazer's doors shut. Then the tires spun for a moment before they dug into the mud and propelled the truck backward. A few clumps of marsh muck flew off the tires and landed in the dry leaves several feet away.

Joel backed the truck around and then pulled forward until he was even with the Bronco. He put it in park and rolled the window down. Allie was in the passenger's seat, trying to push Gunner off the center console so she could see through to Joel and Ben.

"Well, what's the plan?" Joel asked.

Ben hopped off the tailgate and walked to the Joel's window. "You guys follow me out to the road and I'll go over the plan with you there." He smiled. "We're going to set a little trap of our own."

· 9 ·

Joel nodded. "Sounds good. We'll be right behind you."

Ben closed up the box of dynamite and slid it back inside the cargo area of the Bronco. He hated the thought of riding with the stuff, but it was going to give them the upper hand. Besides, he'd already driven with it on the way here.

He'd be checking the contents of any other vehicles he borrowed from now on, he thought as he shook his head.

Ben fired up the Bronco and drove a semicircle around Joel, making a 180-degree turn and heading back toward the trail. He went as fast as he dared but didn't want to push it now that he was aware of his cargo. Each bump and rattle was a tense reminder that there were 40 pounds of impact-sensitive explosives a few feet behind him.

Slowly but surely, they made their way out of the woods, then back along the narrow four-wheel-drive trail. Ben wondered what the kids were thinking as they passed the old Chevy pickup he had scuttled. He hoped they didn't notice the two blood-soaked patches of dirt on the road as they drove over them.

After a few minutes of driving they hit the smoother dirt road and Ben felt a little better about hauling the dynamite. He picked up the pace a bit and headed for the section of road that ran under the first bridge. That would be a good place to stop, out of sight from the quarry and anybody coming over the bridge. There, in the shade, he could go over the plan with Joel and Allie.

Ben glanced down at the radio on the floor to make sure the small red light was still on. It had been silent since he turned it on back in the woods. Looking at his watch, he figured it had only been an hour since he first saw the men at the roadblock.

The two guys in the Bronco had probably radioed over to the quarry with an update after they'd left their friend. Ben figured he still had a little time before the quarry would try to communicate with them.

Ben drove through the intersection and passed by the right-hand turn that led to the highway. Instead, he continued on straight and followed the dirt road, where it veered off toward the river and under the bridge.

As soon as he was in the shade, he pulled off to the side of the road and made a U-turn before parking. Now facing Joel and Allie, he watched them drive in and park on the other side of the road.

"In there, between the columns." Ben pointed to the area between two large concrete support structures.

Joel waved and put the Blazer in gear before backing the truck into the tight, dark spot by the concrete columns and shutting it off.

Ben was already across the dirt road, where he was squatting down near the shoulder and drawing on the ground with a stick. It was dark and cool in the shadows under the bridge and it felt good to be out of the hot sun for a change.

Joel and Allie hurried over to join him. Gunner led the way, ran over to where Ben was kneeling, and lay down, panting on the damp sand. He seemed to appreciate the shade and coolness of the bridge as much as Ben did.

He was glad to see that both Joel and Allie were still carrying their weapons.

"Okay, so what's the plan?" Joel asked.

Ben looked up from his crudely drawn map that showed a rough layout of the two bridges and the highway between them.

"We're here." Ben placed a rock on his drawing. "I want to leave the Blazer here and have you guys take a position up off the highway. Somewhere you have a good view of the bridge. There's a ridge a little up the road from here that looks like a good spot. I'll drop you guys off there so you can be my eyes. I'll set up dynamite on the road in key locations that will provide you with a good defendable position. You can detonate the dynamite bundles by shooting them in case things go wrong and they don't come to me." Ben placed another piece of gravel at that location.

Joel and Allie crouched down and joined him.

"Where will you be?" Joel asked.

"I'm going up the road a bit to set up a spot to ambush them using the rest of the dynamite and the Bronco. I'll signal you with a couple clicks on the radio before I blow the truck." Ben dropped another piece of gravel. "I'll use the radio I found in the Bronco to try to contact them. I'm not sure what I'll say, but something along the lines of needing help. I think I can disguise my voice enough with a little static to pass for one of them. I'll tell them the radio isn't working right or something if they get suspicious. I'm hoping to get them over here."

"But how will we get through the other roadblock?" Allie's eyebrows squished together as she studied the roughly drawn map.

"I'm thinking they'll bring the loader they've been using to move these cars around so they can get across the first bridge. After I deal with them, we can use it to clear a path on the next bridge."

A concerned look crossed Allie's face. "Are you going to kill them?" She swallowed.

Ben was surprised by the question and was tempted to give her a vague answer, but he'd already decided the kids needed to know the truth about things. "These people are killers. I overheard them talking about killing people just like us they had trapped. I can't just leave them here to continue doing this. We have to do the right thing."

"I understand." Allie nodded.

"It's not like they're just going to let us walk out of here anyway," Joel added.

Allie shrugged. "I know, it's just… I don't know. Hard to think about, I guess."

Joel put his hand on Allie's shoulder and looked at her. "Your dad, my mom, my brother, and my sister are all waiting for us. Counting on us. These people? They don't care about us. They only care about themselves."

"He's right." Ben stood. "And I don't like it, either, Allie, but it's literally us or them."

"Okay, what do you need us to do?" Allie asked as she got to her feet.

When Joel got up, Gunner followed, apparently sensing they were moving soon. He headed for the Blazer.

"Gunner, come on, boy. This way," Ben called out.

Gunner paused and gave a confused head tilt in his direction.

"Lock the truck up, will you, Joel? I'll give you guys a ride to your spot."

"Okay." Joel jogged to the Blazer and made his way around the vehicle, locking it as he went. Meanwhile, Allie and Gunner loaded into the Bronco's back seat.

"Just put the other stuff in the back." Ben grabbed his M24 off the back seat and laid it barrel-down into the floor with the butt of the gun resting on the center console.

Allie moved the box of ammo and the other rifle into the back with the crate of dynamite. Gunner was busy sniffing the interior of the truck when Joel yanked open the passenger door and hopped in.

Ben headed back to the intersection but this time made the turn that led up to the highway and the end of the bridge.

Once they were on the main road, he only went a few hundred yards before pulling onto the shoulder. The side of the road went down into a ditch and then rose up in elevation on the other side to the top of a hill that must have been left over from the bridge's construction. The ridge had apparently been there a while because it was thick with vegetation where it ran into the woods.

"Top of that hill." Ben pointed. "Find a spot where you can see across the bridge."

"Got it," Joel answered.

"Radio?" Ben asked as he got out of the truck.

"Got it," Joel repeated and held up the walkie-talkie as he and Allie headed toward the hill. They crossed the half-full ditch, carefully jumping over the dirty water.

Gunner, on the other hand, seemed more than happy to wade right through and run up the other side ahead of them.

Ben opened the back of the Bronco and grabbed 10 yellow sticks out of the wooden crate and gently placed them in his backpack. He paced off what he figured was about 100 yards down the road toward the bridge.

He stopped and looked back at the kids, who were now almost at the wood line on top of the hill. They would have a good vantage point from up there, as well as a good hiding spot. Whoever came over from the quarry should drive right past here. But just in case they stopped, Ben was going to take some precautions.

"Joel, come in. Over." From where he was, Ben watched as Joel brought the radio up to his face.

"Go ahead. Over"

"Let me know when you're ready. I want you to watch me place these. Over." Ben held up one of the dynamite sticks and waved it over his head.

Joel glanced back at him and gave him a thumbs-up as he and Allie joined Gunner in the woods and got out of sight.

Ben looked around for a good place to hide the dynamite. It needed to be hidden from the road but visible to Joel.

"We're ready. Over," Joel said over the radio.

"Let me know if you can see these through your scope as I go. Over." Ben began by putting two sticks together with duct tape and then taping them to the back of a road sign not too far from where the bridge ended. The two sticks together should give Joel an easy target at that distance.

"Can you see it? Over."

"Yes. Over," Joel responded.

Ben repeated this every 10 yards or so, working his way down the shoulder and back toward the kids. He used an old tire, an empty fast food bag, a mile marker sign, and a speed limit sign to hide the other sticks of dynamite.

Joel had five targets in all, and each one had two sticks taped together. That would give Joel some options if things didn't go as planned.

"Looks good. I can see them all. Over."

"Good. Let them pass by and come to me. I want them away from the bridge. These are only in case they stop here or things go south. If that's the case, don't hesitate. Let them have it. Over."

"Roger that. Over."

· 10 ·

Ben kept the radio by his mouth a moment longer. "I'm moving down the road. I'll be just around the corner, not far. I'll let you know when I'm in position and before I do anything. Keep an eye on the bridge and be careful, guys. Over."

"Roger that. Over."

Ben jumped back in the Bronco and headed down the road as he began to go over what he was going to say on the radio. He wanted to keep it brief, that was for sure. He could muffle the radio and fake some interference, so he didn't think the voice mattered as much as what he said.

When he had gone a quarter mile or so up the road, he pulled the truck off to the side and made a small U-turn. He parked the Bronco diagonally across both westbound lanes so the truck was facing in the direction he had just come from. He went around back, opened the tailgate, and threw the extra shotgun ammo in his bag, then grabbed the dead man's rifle case.

Ben pulled the box of dynamite to the center of the cargo area and then out a little toward the tailgate. He thought about keeping a few sticks of dynamite but quickly dismissed the idea and decided it was too dangerous to travel with them. But he did grab the fuse cord out of the box. There was no sense in leaving that behind. They might be able to use it for something. He threw it in the bag with the ammo before continuing around to the passenger's side of the truck to retrieve his M24 from the front seat.

He also wanted to check the glove box for anything of value. He was actually thinking there might be ammo in there for the rifle or maybe another box of shotgun shells.

Ben popped open the glove compartment door and immediately saw he'd been right. A box of ammo. He looked it over. It was a box of .243 WSSM (Winchester Super Short Magnum)-caliber ammunition, and it felt full.

Well, he knew what type of rifle it was now. It was a decent caliber and was worth keeping around as a backup or maybe even to trade for something they needed down the road.

He threw the box of ammo in his bag along with both radios and was about to walk away from the

Bronco when something caught his eye in the glove box.

It looked like a shiny deck of cards but was thicker and held together with a rubber band. But it wasn't a deck of cards. They were drivers' licenses, six of them all together.

Ben shuffled through the blood-stained stack. His heart raced and his blood pressure rose with each flip of the deck as he saw the faces of the victims.

These murderous lowlifes were actually keeping the IDs of the people they killed. And how many others had there been without an ID to steal?

He threw the licenses back into the glove compartment and slammed the door. That was the most disgusting, vile thing he'd seen all day, and he'd seen a lot already.

Ben didn't need another reason to justify what he was about to do. But now, fueled by his grisly find, he walked away from the Bronco recommitted to seeing justice carried out.

He headed toward the woods with a renewed sense of purpose. He couldn't wait to put this place and these people behind him.

Once he was off the road, he looked for a spot that would give him a good vantage point. The woods along the highway sat a couple feet higher than the road itself, so it was just a matter of finding a spot far enough back, but without any vegetation between him and the Bronco, to be out of sight.

He needed a clear shot at the box of dynamite.

He was hoping they would see the Bronco and stop to investigate. But it really didn't matter if they stopped or not—just that they were somewhere close by when he shot the box.

With any luck, they would leave the loader at the roadblock and use a car or truck to get over here. If they drove the loader all the way out here, Ben would have to change the plan. He couldn't risk damaging the big machine with the explosion. He'd have to take them out one by one, no matter how many of them there were.

Ben found a good location between two trees. He set the rifles and the bag down and gathered a few low branches from some nearby saplings. He organized the branches between the trees and settled in behind them. Lying on the ground, he got the M24 in position and looked through the scope at the Bronco. He was only 300 yards away. An easy shot with the .338 Lapua.

Ben sat up and got both radios and his Nalgene bottle out of the bag. He laid the radios side by side in the leaves next to him while he took a much-needed drink. The water wasn't cold but it was wet and felt good on his parched throat. He'd better let the kids know what was going on before he got this underway.

"Joel, come in. Over"

Joel's response was immediate. "Go ahead. Over."

"I'm in position. Any activity on the bridge? Over."

"Negative, don't see anything. Over."

"Roger that. I'm getting ready to kick this thing off. Stay alert and let me know what you see. Over."

"Got it. Over."

Ben put one radio down and picked up the other. He also grabbed some dry leaves with the other hand and held them over the receiver. He paused as he held it in his hand, trying to decide what to say.

Then he took a deep breath and squeezed the call button.

"Having radio trouble. We got 'em at the second bridge. Come quick. Lots of supplies. Need help. Over and out."

The whole time he spoke, he rubbed and crinkled the leaves over the receiver in an effort to simulate heavy static. Ben almost added something about bringing the loader with them but decided it would sound too suspicious and left it out. He hoped they bought it. The plan was set in motion now, and there was no changing it. All he could do was wait for a response.

Ben set the radio down and stared at it for a few

seconds before it crackled to life with a female voice. "Levi says you boys aren't to touch nothin' until we get there. You hear me?"

There was silence followed briefly by another attempt by the same woman to contact Ben's radio. "Hey. You hear me?"

Ben had originally planned on not answering back, regardless of what they said, but he decided to play along a little bit by simply holding the call button down and crunching the leaves into the receiver randomly a couple times.

Then he put the radio down, this time for good. They would figure the radio was out and it would get them over faster—at least, that's what he hoped. He was sure they would be anxious to get here and get in on the score, not wanting the "boys," as the woman on the radio had referred to them, to hoard it for themselves.

People like this didn't care about each other, and he was sure there was no trust within their group.

"Joel, come in. Over."

"Go ahead. Over."

"They're on the way. They took the bait. Get ready. Over."

· 11 ·

Now it was just a matter of time, and all they could do was wait.

"Roger that. I'll let you know what we see. Over," Joel responded.

Ben was proud of Joel for using proper radio etiquette and could tell he was trying his hardest. He'd seen quite a transformation in his son recently.

That didn't keep Ben from second-guessing his decision to leave Joel and Allie up by the bridge alone. He thought that would be the safest place for them, but now his imagination was running wild with possibilities and scenarios where things might not go as planned.

What if there were more than two people coming? He tried to settle down and accept the fact that it was too late to change anything now. They would have to see this plan through, for good or bad. But he reminded himself that he, Joel, and Allie were prepared for this.

Those coming their way were not.

"Dad, come in. There's a loader driving around on the other side of the river. Over."

"Wait! Now there's a car. Over." Joel sounded anxious.

"Okay, keep me posted. Over."

A few minutes passed before he heard from Joel again. "They're both out on the bridge now. The loader is moving the cars out of the way. Over."

"Just two of them? Over."

"Yeah. The car is just sitting there, waiting."

"Let me know when they get through. Over."

"Roger that. Over."

Ben looked through his scope one more time and stared at the wooden crate filled with dynamite. He couldn't help but wonder if he should have taken a chance and attempted to blow the roadblock open.

Was it worth the risk to deal with these people? Or was he letting his pride get in the way of their safety and his making practical decisions?

He shook his head as he thought about it. No, he was doing the right thing. He had thought this through, and it was time to put any doubts aside and get ready to end this.

"Two more vehicles pulled out of the quarry. They're heading this way! Over."

"That's okay. Stick to the plan. Over."

"Looks like a pickup and a small dump truck. Over."

"Roger that. Over."

Ben had a feeling the dying man's last words were as worthless as he was. This was precisely why Ben had laid the trap the way he had. As long as they all came to him and were close together, it wouldn't matter if there were 100 of them. He just hoped he had been convincing enough on the radio for them to buy into the plan.

The last thing he wanted was for the people to get off the bridge and split up.

"The loader moved the last car. They're through the roadblock. Loader is parking across both lanes blocking the bridge. Now the driver is out and getting into the first car. Here they come. Over."

"Good. Let me know when they pass your position. Over." Ben was that this part, at least, was going to plan.

The loader was crucial to them getting out of here, and he'd been afraid they might drive it all the way over to him. He didn't want the loader anywhere near the explosion for fear the blast would destroy it. A ruined loader wouldn't be the end of the world, but it would mean going all the way back over to the quarry and having to find another working loader to use.

That was time Ben would rather spend putting miles between them and this place. He was already disappointed at the amount of time this whole ordeal had cost them.

Please, God, let this go as planned. Ben took a few deep breaths and got ready for what was about to go down.

"They're all coming, but the car is way out in front of the others. Going fast. It's a guy and a woman. Over," Joel said on the radio.

"Roger that. Over." It must have been the woman on the radio, and Levi, who Ben presumed was the leader of this sick bunch of criminals.

"The car is passing us now. Pickup and dump truck not far behind. Over."

Ben turned the volume down on both handheld radios. Hopefully the man and woman wouldn't get here too far ahead of the others. He needed them all in the same spot for this to work.

"Pickup and dump truck passing now. Over."

"Roger that. Now sit tight until you hear from me. Over." Ben's eyes were fixed on the road as he waited for the first vehicle to come around the bend.

He didn't have to wait long before he could hear the rumble of a vehicle approaching. It was a black Trans Am with a big gold eagle on the hood. An older woman smoked a cigarette in the driver's seat. Next to her in the passenger's seat sat a man who looked about the same age.

They began to slow down, and Ben was sure they had spotted the Bronco sitting in the middle of the road. Then the Trans Am stopped moving altogether and parked. The pair was talking back and forth until the man motioned with his hand for the woman to keep going.

They slowly approached the Bronco and parked about 10 feet away. Neither one got out of the car immediately. The man held the radio up to his face, and Ben heard him instantly come through on the radio next to him.

"Where are you guys? We're here at the truck. Come in." There was a long pause before he continued. "I thought you were at the bridge. What's goin' on?"

Ben watched through his scope as the man grew visibly frustrated and eventually threw the radio down. He swung the door open on the Trans Am and pulled himself up and out by the door. Standing there for a minute, he looked around suspiciously at the woods on both sides of the road.

The woman joined him, getting out of the car on her side.

They both turned as the pickup came into view, followed by the small dump truck. The pickup drove up next to the Trans Am and parked. A middle-aged man got out right away and walked to the front of his truck and stood. He looked at the Bronco before turning to the older couple.

"Well, where are they?" Ben heard him ask.

"No idea, and they ain't answering the radio." The older man threw his hands up and turned to watch as the dump truck came to a stop.

The guy driving the truck didn't bother getting out and instead leaned out the window. "Where are they?"

The pickup driver shook his head and walked toward them. He looked in the front seat first and then made his way around the back. "Nothing in here but the box of dynamite."

"I told them not to take the whole box! Idiots. Grab that and bring it here, will you?"

Ben tensed up as the guy grabbed the wooden crate out of the back of the Bronco. It had to feel a little lighter, but the guy didn't act like anything was amiss as he walked toward the Trans Am and the dump truck.

"Give me the keys so I can open the trunk. I left mine in the loader," the driver of the Trans am yelled.

The woman tossed the keys in his direction but missed him by a mile. Ben heard him curse as he walked to where the keys had landed.

Meanwhile, the guy carrying the dynamite shook his head and set the wooden crate down by the rear tire of the Trans Am.

"You put it in the trunk. I'm going up to the next bridge to see if they're up there," the pickup driver said.

"I'll follow you," the dump truck driver called out.

Ben couldn't believe what just happened. Here, he had been worried about getting them close to the dynamite. Now it was sitting on the ground in the middle of them all.

Ben thumbed the radio call button twice and took aim. He thought about the faces on the stack of bloody licenses as he pulled the trigger.

· 12 ·

BOOM!

The shock wave from the explosion passed over Ben as the ground shook. He instinctively curled up and covered his head and ears with his arms.

Seconds after the explosion, dirt and gravel showered him. The sound of the explosion still echoed in the distance like rolling thunder. He brushed himself off and looked up to survey the damage. The devastation was awe-inspiring.

The remains of the Trans Am and the pickup truck lay intertwined and burning in the median some 50 yards from where they had been parked. Both vehicles were unrecognizable and completely destroyed.

The dump truck fared better but not by much. It was pushed back 20 or 30 yards and had much of its cab blown off. Metal parts littered the highway like crumpled-up pieces of paper, some of them still burning. The only recognizable piece remaining of the truck was the solid steel dump body.

The Bronco was badly damaged and lay on its side. Although not totally destroyed, it had some serious body damage from rolling over several times and was beyond salvaging.

Ben got off the ground and brushed more dirt and bits of asphalt from his hair. He quickly gathered his gear and headed back to the road.

As he got closer, he could see he'd made the right choice in not using the dynamite to deal with the roadblock. Ben eyed the crater left by the explosion. The dynamite had blasted a hole through several layers of blacktop to the dirt below. The hole in the road almost spanned the entire width of the westbound lanes. The explosion would have destroyed the bridge or at the very least made it too unstable and risky to cross.

He dug the radio out of the bag and reached out to Joel. "How about coming to get me in the truck so we can get out of here? Over."

"We heard it! On our way. Over."

A wave of conscience hit Ben. He had just blown four people up. He looked around for bodies. He doubted there was much left of the older couple or the pickup driver but thought the guy in the dump truck might be around somewhere.

He walked around the wrecked vehicles for a few minutes as he surveyed the damage a little closer. If there were any remains or bodies, he'd like to find them before the kids got there. But there were none to be found, and before long he heard the familiar exhaust note of the approaching Blazer.

Joel stopped the Blazer well outside the blast zone and got out of the truck. He had a look of astonishment on his face. "Wow! That was a big explosion!"

He eyed the damaged vehicles. Allie hopped out of the truck on her side but stopped before she closed the door and held her hand up to a whining Gunner. "Stay here, boy. There's too much stuff on the ground."

Gunner reluctantly sat down in the passenger's seat and hung his head out the open window.

"That really did a lot of damage. We could feel it from where we were," Joel said, his eyes wide.

"Yeah, well, that was a lot of dynamite," Ben said.

"So… I guess they're all dead?" Allie tentatively eyed the remains of the dump truck as she walked past.

"Don't feel sorry for them, Allie. They were terrible people. Murderers." Ben thought about the licenses again. "I found more evidence in the Bronco to confirm that. Trust me when I say the world is a better place without them."

"At least other people will be able to travel through here safely," she said.

"That's right. Who knows? It could be us. We may end up coming back this way at some point. You never know." Carrying his gear, Ben headed for the Blazer but handed off the newly acquired hunting rifle to Joel.

"What is it?" Joel asked.

"A .243 short mag," Ben answered.

Joel partially unzipped the soft case and peeked in at the rifle. "Looks nice."

"Yeah, it's in good shape. I found a box of ammo for it also. It's there in my bag. I figured it was too nice to leave, and it may come in handy down the road."

"Cool." Joel zipped the case up and headed to the truck as he took one more look around at the aftermath of the dynamite.

Allie had already started walking back to the Blazer but Ben and Joel quickly caught up to her. She was standing on the shoulder of the road and staring up in silence.

"What is it?" Joel asked.

Allie remained silent and frozen in her tracks for a moment before she pointed up into a nearby tree.

There, some 20 feet off the ground, hung the body of the dump truck driver. The corpse was draped over a large limb, its appendages dangling like those of a rag doll. One of the legs was missing from the knee down. All that remained in its place were dangling ribbons of flesh.

Ben was glad the body had at least landed so that the face wasn't visible. He hadn't even noticed it when he was searching earlier—not that he could have done anything to hide the body, even if he had seen it.

Joel put his arm across Allie's shoulders and forced her away from the gruesome scene with a gentle whisper. "Come on. Let's go."

· 13 ·

Ben was worried by the blank expression on her face. Was this death and destruction going to be too much for her to cope with? Other than following Joel's lead and heading for the truck, Allie didn't respond. She didn't say anything until they got back to the Blazer and greeted Gunner with strained enthusiasm. "Hey there! Did you miss me?"

Gunner wagged his tail and hopped into the back seat, where he anxiously waited for her to climb in and join him, which she did.

Ben and Joel loaded the gear into the truck as they talked out their next steps.

"So how about you run me back to the loader and then follow me to the next bridge? It shouldn't take too long to clear a path and we'll be on our way." Ben took a big drink from his water bottle.

"Sounds good to me. Do you know how to drive one of those things?" Joel asked.

"Yeah, it's been a while, but I'll manage." Ben got situated in the passenger seat while Joel got back behind the wheel and started the truck.

"I still can't believe how loud that explosion was," Allie chimed in from the back seat.

"You could probably hear that for miles," Joel added.

"Yeah, that was pretty impressive," Allie said.

Ben was glad Allie was back with them and at least engaging in conversation again. He didn't dare confess his fears that the explosion could have possibly drawn too much attention to their location. There was no need to bring it up anyway. They already had enough of a reason to keep things moving and get out of there.

Ben ached all over. He was close to pushing his physical limit for the day and exhausted from the morning's activities. The only thing keeping him going was his determination to save the day from being a total loss.

But for as hard as he was pushing himself and the kids, the day still seemed to be slipping away impossibly fast. It was already past noon, and they still had a lot of work ahead of them before they could get back on the road.

Providing everything went well with the loader, he hoped they could be underway in an hour. Maybe less. That might give them a few hours of actual driving time. They'd throw in a pit stop for gas and he'd consider it a success to get into Illinois tonight and find a good, safe place to sleep.

"How far do you think we'll get today?" Allie asked.

She must have noticed him looking at his watch. "A hundred miles or so into Illinois, with any luck." Ben turned in his seat to face her for a second. "We'll be really close to Pittsburgh by the end of the day tomorrow."

Allie forced a crooked little smile, but uncertainty danced in her eyes.

He smiled back, hoping to reassure her, and turned to face the road again. He didn't blame her for having doubts and knew she had to process this in her own way. So would Joel, for that matter. Ben knew he couldn't hide all the bodies.

The loader was parked sideways across the bridge with its massive front bucket resting on top of the concrete lane divider. The old faded yellow four-wheel drive model had long ago lost its emblems. The paint was peeling off in several areas, revealing a rust-pitted finish underneath.

It was the worst-looking piece of equipment Ben had ever seen.

He grabbed the radio and started to get out of the truck before Joel had a chance to come to a complete stop. "Wait until I get it started before you take off."

"I thought you wanted us to follow you?" Joel asked.

"No, that's fine." Ben hopped out of the truck. "I'm thinking you and Allie can go on up ahead and maybe make us some lunch, if you don't mind. It's going to take me a while to get there in that thing. And it'll probably take at least half an hour to clear the roadblock. If we eat now, maybe we can push on a little longer this evening. Just keep your radio on."

"Will do."

Ben closed the truck door as Allie was climbing into the passenger's seat. He walked toward the loader. The front bucket was equipped with larger-than-standard metal forks. They had welded additional metal to the fork ends to make each one about three feet longer than the original length. He figured they must have done this to make moving the cars around easier.

Ben climbed up the rusty, bent metal treads to the cab and opened the door. He was relieved to see the keys hanging in the ignition.

If the driver had kept the keys on him, they might have never found them after the blast. With the way this thing was parked, they would have been trapped all over again without a way to move it.

He sat down in the torn, duct-taped seat and felt it sink down on its struts as he turned the key to the halfway position. As soon as the glow plug indicator lit up, he turned the key the rest of the way. The big diesel engine roared to life and spewed a big puff of black smoke from the stack.

Ben looked at the Blazer and gave Joel a thumbs-up before he pulled the cab door shut. Joel finished the U-turn he'd started making when they first got there and headed toward the second bridge.

Ben cut the wheel hard to the left and put the loader in reverse. The front bucket scraped along the top of the concrete divider before he had a chance to lift it with the joystick.

"Oops," he muttered. While he was lifting the bucket out of the way, the loader came to an abrupt stop as one of the rear tires made contact with a minivan that had been part of the roadblock. Ben grimaced and shook his head. He took a deep breath and tried to calm down.

He was rushing and he needed to slow down before he went any further. The weariness of the day was setting in.

Nice and easy, he thought. *Bucket up, wheel turned.*

The loader crept forward slowly as he feathered the gas pedal. The articulated steering was something he needed to get used to, but the controls were similar to the loader he had driven in the army, and before long, he had it straightened out and was heading down the road.

He pushed the gear selection lever by the steering column into the highway position and felt the lurch of the transmission as it shifted into a higher gear set.

No surprise that only a few of the gauges worked in the old loader, so Ben had no idea how fast he was going, but it felt painfully slow. He mashed the pedal down as far as it would go, trying to coax as much speed out of the old equipment as possible.

As the engine raced, he looked back and saw thick black smoke pouring out of the exhaust stack. He quickly backed off on the throttle, not wanting to push too hard.

Better to get there slow than not at all. The last thing he wanted to do was go to the quarry and get another loader. That might not even be an option, though. This was most likely the only working piece of heavy equipment they had. He'd seen newer equipment in the yard, but it was probably non-operable due to the EMP, just like most everything else.

The only working gauge seemed to be the temperature indicator, which was steadily rising. Ben backed off a little more on the gas pedal and anxiously glanced between the gauge and the road for a few minutes.

Eventually the little needle dropped out of the red zone on the gauge and stabilized at an acceptable engine temperature. Ben breathed a tepid sigh of relief.

He just needed this old rust bucket to hold together a little while longer.

· 14 ·

By the time Ben reached the second bridge, Joel
and Allie had the stove out and were boiling water.
Joel had the Blazer parked off the road in the shade
of some trees at the wood line.

Ben was glad to see they were on the opposite
side of the road from where he'd hid the first body.
Then he wondered if that was why they were
parked on that side.

Joel had the AR set up on the hood of the truck
and was throwing a stick for Gunner while Allie
watched. They all paused and looked as Ben came
around the bend in the loader. It had taken him
more than 15 minutes to get there and he didn't
want to waste any more time. He headed right to
the massive pile of cars and got to work.

He started at the top of the pile and worked his
way down, only moving the cars far enough to
make a narrow path the loader could fit through.
The extended forks made it easy to get under the

cars and move them around, and the process was taking less time than he thought. In spite of his concerns, the loader seemed to be holding up okay. He began to think he would drive it across the bridge ahead of the kids, just in case they encountered any more blockages.

"Hey, Dad. Lunch is ready. Over."

Ben barely heard the radio over the growl of the engine as he revved it up, trying to maximize the RPMs and provide ample power to the hydraulics that worked the front bucket. The loader didn't have the power to lift more than one car at a time, which made clearing the roadblock a tedious job. There were only a few cars left, though, and he wanted to finish before he dared shut the loader down.

"Go ahead and eat. I want to finish up here. Hey, listen, when you're done, eating will you empty the spare fuel tanks into the truck? Over."

"Okay, no problem. Over."

That should buy them another hour of drive time in case they couldn't find a suitable place to fill up right away.

Ben put the radio down and got back to work. He was hungry, but the last few cars on the bottom of the pile were crushed badly. It was taking all of his concentration to get the cars untangled from one another and move them from the road.

He finally got the last crumpled car balanced in the forks, and he drove through to the other side of the roadblock for the first time. Depositing the car to the side, he made a tight U-turn and drove back through the narrow clearing.

If the loader could get through, they should have no problem in the Blazer.

While he'd been moving the last few cars, he'd noticed the bridge was clear all the way to the other side. They wouldn't need the loader after all, which was good news. He pulled off the road and onto the grass near the Blazer before he shut the loader down. Almost as an afterthought, he decided to take keys to the loader with him.

You never know, he thought as he plucked them out of the ignition.

If there were any more quarry people left, he didn't want to leave them with the ability to set this trap up again. And then there was the very real possibility they'd be coming back this way and it might come in handy.

He couldn't see them staying in Maryland. Regardless of how much his ex fought him on it, he was going to insist they return to Colorado. He knew how to live off the land there, and he had a good setup at the house.

But no point in worrying about that yet. He'd have to cross that bridge when he got there, and for right now, he just wanted to get across this one.

He climbed down the steps from the cab and then jumped the last couple feet to the ground, causing his whole body to ache and making him realize how sore he was.

Gunner trotted over and met him on his way to the Blazer. He gave the dog a pat on the head. Allie had a warm pouch of food and a fresh water bottle waiting for him on the tailgate of the truck.

"We refilled some of the bottles from the river," she said.

"Good idea and thank you." Ben sat down on the tailgate and took a moment before he started to eat.

"No problem. Just trying to save us some time." Allie shrugged as she headed back to the front of the truck, where Joel was.

Ben took a breath. It felt good to sit still for a change. The shock absorbers under the loader seat were worn out, much like the loader itself. He'd felt every bump and jolt while he was moving the cars and he was glad to be finished. The vibrations from the diesel engine still lingered like a fading itch as he ate.

Ben quickly finished the rehydrated macaroni and cheese and cleaned up using some of the filtered water. He hadn't realized how filthy he was until he used a little soap to wash his hands and face. It would be nice if they could stay somewhere near a fairly clean water source tonight. After the day he had, he'd like to clean himself up the rest of the way.

But water or no water, one thing was certain: wherever they stayed, they had to keep it simple and low key. He wasn't taking any chances tonight, and the only thing he planned on doing, other than getting washed up a little more, was setting up his tent. He'd leave dinner up to the kids, if they made anything at all.

But to set up camp anywhere else, they had to get some driving time in first, and getting away from here was something he was very keen to do.

"Well, you guys ready?" Ben asked.

"Yep," Allie chirped.

"Way ahead of you." Joel was already packing up the AR. Allie and Gunner loaded into the truck while Joel stashed the gun in the back.

"How about you drive for a while?" Ben asked.

"Yeah, sure, no problem. We almost have a full tank since I added the fuel from the cans," Joel answered.

"Excellent! We can get a few solid hours of driving in before we have to stop, then," Ben said.

"Sounds good to me." Allie nodded. "Let's get out of here!"

· 15 ·

Ben settled into his seat as Joel pulled out of their shady parking spot and onto the road. The pile of cars seemed so much taller now that he wasn't sitting up high in the loader.

The cars he hadn't moved were still stacked three high on both sides of the narrow passage and blocked out the sun as they passed by. Puddles of fluids lay everywhere on the ground, and they looked like a mixture of gas, antifreeze, and motor oil.

His doing, he knew. In his haste, he'd missed his aim with the long sharp forks on the loader and skewered more than a few of the cars as he moved them.

"Slow down a little. I don't want this stuff splashing all over the truck," Ben said.

"What is it?" Joel asked.

"Mostly fuel. A lot of the cars were leaking." Ben watched as they passed the last of the roadblock.

91

Once out on the open bridge, Joel picked up speed and headed over the Mississippi River. The churning brown water moved swiftly below them. Ben watched the currents of the river as they swirled into miniature whirlpools and then faded away. He felt like he was in a trance and had to force himself to look up at the road.

They had to stay alert through here. The bridge ended in what looked like a pretty congested area on the map. They would have to go through a section of the downtown area before they could pick up a route south and get back to I-70. This was exactly the kind of place they were trying to avoid.

"When you get to the end of the bridge, take the first right onto 143. That follows the river south where it runs into 3. We want to take that back to I-70. It looks like the best way back to the interstate."

"No problem. I can handle it, if you want to sleep or rest in the back," Joel offered.

"I'm fine. I think we should still stop at the usual time today, even though we got a late start. There's no reason to wear ourselves out and end up making a mistake." Ben glanced out the window and enjoyed the breeze as it cooled him down.

At the end of the bridge, there was a small marina and a few industrial buildings. All seemed calm and there was nobody in sight.

A few minutes later, Joel made the right onto Route 143 and headed south along the river.

At this point, burned-down buildings and houses were a common sight. The vandalized and busted-up storefronts all began to seem like a normal part of the landscape. And this town was no different from anything else they'd seen so far.

Still, though, Ben was hoping that, closer to the middle of the country, they would find a few areas that hadn't suffered the same fate as these other places— maybe a few small pockets of semi-normal society.

So far, there was no evidence that anything close to normal remained. Everything they had seen had all been about the same. Of course, areas of little or no population looked okay at first glance, but the houses were dark and the streets all had that ghost-town feel to them. You knew there were people watching, but nobody showed themselves. The occasional curtain would move or door crack open to watch them pass.

But for the most part, people seemed to be keeping to themselves. Based on their experience so far on this trip, that was probably for the best.

Eight days had passed since the EMPs detonated, and without supplies, people everywhere would really start to suffer.

The human body could go weeks without food if necessary, but water was another story. Within three to four days, the effects of dehydration would begin to set in. Not many people could last over a week without clean, drinkable water.

And the majority of the population—like Allie's dad—lived in urban areas, where they needed electricity to access water. Ben tried to push that thought from his mind.

There had been no warning before the attacks, so there had been no time for anyone to stock up or prepare in any way. People would be left with what food and water they had on hand, and for the average household, it wouldn't be enough to last very long. Ultimately, people would become desperate and attempt to drink water from any source they could find.

That would only compound their dilemma in the long run. They might be okay for a day or two at the most, but eventually, gastrointestinal illness of some sort would set in. Their bodies would be depleted of even more fluids, leaving them in worse shape than before they'd drunk the tainted water.

A myriad of diseases could be introduced to the human body through water-borne bacteria, and without medical care, they would be fatal.

Ben couldn't help but wonder if that would be the largest killer in all this. How many people were weak and helpless already? How many lives would *E. coli* or some other bacterial illness claim? Those quiet, dark houses they passed quite possibly held people with failing organs and dehydrated bodies hanging on by a thread.

He could imagine them waiting for the mercy of death as the only means of release from their torment. There was no one coming to save them.

What a wretched world they lived in now, where survival was a daily challenge.

Joel steered the Blazer onto Route 3 and continued following the river south toward the interstate. The road hugged the contours of the winding river more closely now, and Ben soon found himself staring out the window as he caught glimpses of the muddy water through the trees.

Once again, the churning water lulled him into a trance, and his thoughts drifted to Emma and Bradley. His lids felt heavy as he wondered how they were making out and how his ex was taking care of them. He hoped they were at their grandfather's and safe from the horrors of all this.

He tried to hang onto that thought as he drifted off to sleep.

· 16 ·

Joel was glad to see his dad asleep. It had been a big day and he had gotten them out of yet another jam. Joel knew it had taken its toll on him, and he'd noticed the look of exhaustion on his father's face back at the bridge.

As usual, Joel wished he could have helped more, but at least he was able to drive, allowing his dad time to rest.

Hopefully, they wouldn't run into any trouble and could get back onto the interstate soon. The road they were on was in decent shape, but lots of turns and blind corners made it tricky. Not knowing what was up ahead forced him to drive at a slower speed than what he wanted to.

He glanced in the rearview mirror, wishing Allie was up front with him, but he wasn't about to wake his dad up so they could switch places. With any luck, his dad would sleep until they had to stop for gas.

Joel couldn't help but feel a little guilty about pushing to go duck hunting last night. He wasn't convinced it had caused their situation this morning, but he wasn't sure it hadn't, either.

His dad said he thought they'd closed the bridge off behind them as soon as they'd crossed over it yesterday, so Joel wasn't sure why he felt somewhat responsible, but he did.

They were lucky they hadn't been found last night while they were sleeping. Joel didn't want to think about what those guys would have done to them.

A road sign up ahead listed a few destinations and their distances in mileage. Ten more miles to go until they reached the interstate.

Joel checked on Allie in the rearview mirror again. She was still quietly looking out the window. Occasionally she would divert her attention away from the passing landscape just long enough to appease Gunner with a few seconds of attention. She was clearly in deep thought, and Joel wasn't sure if he should say anything or not.

After a few more minutes, his desire to talk to her won out and he couldn't remain silent any longer. "Are you okay?"

A few seconds passed before Allie answered. "Yeah, I'm...um... I just can't really believe this is all real sometimes. I mean, I know it's real, but I guess I just don't want to accept it. Do you know what I mean?" Allie brushed her hair out of her face as she looked up at the rearview mirror.

Joel looked back at her. "I know exactly what you mean. I think I feel the same way." He quickly turned around to focus on the road, contenting himself with watching her in the mirror.

She let out a little sigh. "It's like, just when I start to get to the point where I can accept what's going on, something else happens. I had no idea there would be so many people out to get us. I mean, just a week ago I was at the movies with my friends, and we walked around downtown afterward and got some coffee at the Steaming Bean. That all seems so far away now, like a whole other lifetime. I'm afraid those are the memories that won't seem real anymore. I don't want to replace those times with this." She looked out the window as they made their way around another multicar pileup on the road.

It was as if Gunner could sense Allie's frustration. He sat up in the seat next to her and began to lean in, pressing his head into her chest. She put her arm around him and scratched his head.

"It's okay, boy. It's okay. Sorry about that," she sighed.

Joel understood her completely. "It's okay. I know what you mean. I can't stop thinking about all the things I'll probably never get to do. I can't believe I'm saying this, but I'd give anything to go back to school in a couple months. Do you think we'll ever go to school or anything like that again, or are we just supposed to be adults now?" He sped up as he came into a straight section of road.

"I don't know, but whatever happens, I know it'll never be the same again," Allie answered.

They rode in silence for a few miles until Joel saw the exit sign for the interstate.

"We made it back to the interstate. Thank God! I'm ready to get off this road." Joel readjusted himself in his seat, sitting up a little straighter as he steered the Blazer around the long curve of the exit ramp onto I-70 east.

The smoke cloud from St. Louis still hung heavy in the air. Taking this route back to the interstate was shorter but brought them close to where they had been the other day.

Joel thought about the first bridge they'd tried to cross and the plane that had taken it out. The pungent burnt odor was just as bad as he remembered it being yesterday. The strong smell and thick air spoiled what little pleasure Joel had squeezed from getting back to the main road.

At least they were heading away from the smoke this time.

"We'll be in Pittsburgh in no time." Joel glanced back at Allie. He expected a smile, but Allie had a concerned look on her face instead. "Hey, you okay?"

"Joel, I'm worried. Well, not so much worried, I guess, but scared."

"Of what?" he asked.

"About what we'll find in Pittsburgh. If we do find my dad, I don't want to stay there. I want to stay with you guys. My dad can't take care of us, and I don't want to risk never seeing you again."

Joel felt flush as the blood rushed to his face. He felt the same way she did but had been afraid to say anything before now. He was worried he would come off as being selfish. After all, she had already lost her mom. Who was he to keep her from being with her dad? But apparently, she felt the same way he did.

"I don't want you to stay in Pittsburgh, either," Joel confessed.

Allie smiled at him in the rearview mirror. Then the smile vanished and she shook her head. "I don't want me or my dad to be a burden on you guys. It's not fair to you or your dad. You need to get to your mom and brother and sister."

"We'll figure something out." The words came out of Joel's mouth, but in reality, he had no idea how that was going to work. He repeated it again to convince himself more than anything. "We'll figure something out."

· 17 ·

The first thing Ben noticed when he woke up was how fast they were going.

How long had he been asleep? They must have made it back to the interstate. He rubbed his head where it had been leaning against the metal of the doorframe. It hadn't made a great pillow, and he thought he probably would have slept a little longer if it wasn't for the hard steel vibrating against his skull.

"Hey, you're up," Joel said.

"Yeah. Where are we? How long have I been asleep?" he asked.

Allie leaned forward. "You were out for a couple hours. We're right about here." She handed the map to Ben and showed him where they were.

"We're below half a tank also," Joel added. "We better find a place to stop soon."

Ben nodded, still studying the map.

Joel leaned over and pointed at the map. "Looks like a nice river there. Might be a good place to stop for the night."

"Kaskaskia River," Ben read out loud. "Never heard of it, but it looks like it might have some possibilities. Could be another hour away with a fuel stop thrown in there." He held his finger on one location of the map and his thumb on the other, trying to scale the distance based on what they had already traveled.

Still a little groggy from his nap, he rubbed his eyes and checked his watch. "That should be doable now that we're back on the interstate. You good to keep going?"

"Yep."

"All right." After few more minutes, Ben was fully awake, and although his neck was a little sore from sleeping against the doorframe, he felt rested.

He briefly considered the possibility of switching out with Joel after they got gas and then driving past their usual stopping time. But the more he thought it over, the less it seemed like a good idea.

It just wasn't wise to push it, especially in the dark. It would only take one mistake and a split-second of bad decision-making to end the whole trip.

No, they would fill up the tanks and stop at the Kaskaskia River for the night. The two-hour nap had given him a boost of energy, but it wouldn't last and they all needed a solid night's sleep. They could get a proper start to the day tomorrow and, with any luck, end up just outside Pittsburgh by the end of the day if it went well.

Ben was eager to reach his kids, but he had promised Allie to get her to her dad, so he tried to remain focused on that as the main goal for now. If they we fortunate enough to find her father, Ben imagined she would want to stay with him.

It would be hard on Joel, but they had to press on to Maryland if they ever wanted to see Bradley and Emma again, not to mention Joel's mom and grandfather.

Even though Joel's relationship with his mom had been strained lately, Ben was sure they would both be happy to see each other. It would be all right with Ben, on the other hand, if he never saw her again.

But he tried to remind himself that, regardless of what he thought about Casey and her choices, she was still the children's mother. There would be plenty of time to worry about that later, though. They were just about at the halfway point of their journey, and if the second half was anything like the first, they would have their work cut out for them.

Pittsburgh alone would present enough of a challenge. Ben had already decided they would leave the Blazer outside the city and hike in.

The vehicle would attract too much attention, and they wouldn't have to risk damaging the truck in what he expected would resemble a war zone. The trek would take longer on foot, but he was convinced it was the way to go.

If Pittsburgh was like most of the places they'd been through, they would have to make their way into the city building by building until they got to her dad's. At this point, he was leaning toward a nighttime insertion.

Although at night the city would be just as dangerous, if not more so, they stood a better chance at getting in and out unnoticed. Cover was important, because they all had to go. He needed Allie to direct him to her dad's, and he was going to need Joel and Gunner to watch his back.

He didn't like the thought of leaving the Blazer alone, but they'd cover it up with the netting and some brush like before, and it should be fine. The well-being of the Blazer would be the least of his concerns once they were in the city.

Then Ben had a troubling thought. What if they did find Allie's dad and he was in bad shape? If he was as inept and helpless as Allie claimed, Ben couldn't very well leave her or her dad there and have a clear conscience about it.

Ben had grown fond of Allie and he could tell Joel was falling head over heels for her, to say the least. What kind of father would he be if he left her behind with grim prospects for survival? At this point, he might need Allie to stay with them for Joel's sake, if not for all the other reasons why it was the right thing to do.

He needed Joel as healthy and mentally fit as possible, and Ben was certain that having Allie along with them was a key part of his son's well-being. They were good for each other, for that matter.

Ben even had a hard time imagining the truck without her in it. He felt like they had bonded, and the more he got to know her, the more he saw in her that he liked.

Like the way she'd interacted with the Jon's little girl, Jessie, back in Kansas. Allie had just been kidnapped at gunpoint hours earlier, and there she was, selflessly trying to comfort a little girl she had just met.

If Allie had decided to sit sullen in the back seat and not say a word the whole trip, he couldn't have faulted her for what she'd been through so far. But she hadn't and she wasn't. She remained positive in spite of all the good reasons not to.

Allie might also be a good persuader to get Emma to come back to Colorado with them if it came to that. He could imagine the two girls getting along really well. Allie could be a good role model and friend for Emma in a world that didn't afford those luxuries anymore.

Ben couldn't imagine being in any of the kids' shoes right now—having their whole lives in front of them, all their hopes and dreams for the future snuffed out by something beyond their control. Devastating.

And Allie losing her mom at the start of it all and having to go through the first couple days completely alone? The girl had character in spades—that was for sure.

Ben suddenly felt ashamed of himself for even considering parting ways with her in Pittsburgh. His mind was made up. Allie and her dad were coming with them.

Four people and a dog would be tight in the Blazer. They would have to move some things around, but they could make it work.

When they got to Maryland, they would have to figure out something else. They would need a bigger truck or maybe a small tow-behind camper. Pulling extra weight would be slow going, but the Blazer could tow a small camper with no trouble.

Ben would have to think it through a while, but they'd come up with something by then. After all, there was strength in numbers, and even if Allie's dad was clueless about survival, he sounded like a smart guy otherwise. They could teach him a few things as they went. And having an extra set of hands around couldn't hurt.

Of course, that also meant another mouth to feed. That was one part of this equation he couldn't ignore. He and Joel were going to have to step up the hunting and fishing in order to sustain them. They were doing well so far with the supplies they'd brought, but he'd never expected them to last forever.

The bag of dog food he'd found was a godsend and would keep Gunner fed for a couple weeks, at least.

Joel tapped the dash. "I hope we find a place soon. We're getting low."

Ben leaned over and looked at the gas gauge. "We'll be all right. There's gotta be a place soon."

Unfortunately, they couldn't be picky about where they stopped this time. The spare cans were empty, and they would have to settle for the next gas station they came to, regardless of what it looked like.

· 18 ·

Ben felt guilty for sleeping now and realized they probably would have stopped before they got this low on gas if he had been awake. It wasn't Joel's fault; he most likely hadn't wanted to wake Ben and was only trying to be considerate by letting him rest. But now they were in a bad position—one Ben had avoided until now.

Allie rubbed Gunner's side as he lay stretched out across the rear bench seat with his head in her lap. "Are we going to be okay?"

"Yeah, we'll be fine. We can squeeze in another 30 miles with what we have left in the tank." Ben tried to sound confident, but in truth he was a little concerned. He wasn't so much worried about being able to find a place to gas-up; he was sure they'd see a gas station soon. His real concern was *where* they stopped.

They drove on in silence for a few minutes as everyone seemed to focus on the search for a place

FALLOUT

to fuel up. Even Gunner seemed to join in as he sat upright next to Allie.

"There!" Joel pointed to a road with a gas station symbol on it. "Two and a half miles to gas, next exit."

"Good. See, we're fine." Ben looked at Gunner, who had transformed from passed out and snoring on Allie's lap to sitting upright and panting loudly. "That dog always knows when something's going on, I swear." Ben shook his head and turned around.

Allie nodded in agreement. "He does seem to have a sixth sense, doesn't he?"

Joel snorted. "He's too smart for his own good."

The mood seemed lighter in the truck as they drove. Maybe it was the fact they had found a place to fill up, or maybe it was the promise of a chance to stretch their legs.

Either way, the lightness was a welcome change from the dreary funk that seemed to follow them from Missouri.

Joel took the next exit and steered around a burned-out bread truck blocking the exit lane. They had to go off the shoulder and around through the grass. Joel made the maneuver a little too fast and Gunner slid across the seat, pinning Allie to the side of the truck.

"Slow it down there, Speed Racer." She laughed.

"Sorry. I didn't think the shoulder went down that far." Joel shrugged apologetically and wrangled the truck back onto the asphalt.

Ben shook his head and gave Joel a look.

"What? I'm sorry." Joel smiled.

They regained their composure and got off the exit as the road opened up into a small retail area with several gas stations and chain restaurants lining both sides of the road.

"Well, it looks like we have lots of choices," Joel said.

"Let's go to the one farthest down on the left." Ben pointed at a small convenience store at the far end of the developed area.

It was a good quarter mile off the interstate and looked like the best choice. They could keep an eye on most of the other buildings at the exit as well as on the interstate. Ben normally would have insisted in pushing on to a less developed area to get gas, but they didn't have that option right now.

They all stared as Joel drove them past the burned-out shells of buildings and trashed stores. The signs out front were the only indications of what the stores once sold.

It was an odd sight to see the well-manicured landscaping around the entrances that led to large piles of charred rubble.

The remaining buildings showed the usual scars left by looters and thieves. Bits of trash and rubble were randomly scattered around the empty parking lots. Some lighter pieces of trash fluttered across the street in front of them on a warm gust of wind.

The place looked like it belonged in a late-night horror flick.

Joel pulled into the last gas station at the end of the street and did the required loop around the building. Without too much trouble, they found the underground tank access lids near the front of the lot and quickly got set up to pump fuel.

Allie insisted on doing her part and taking a turn at the pump. Joel helped her get the hose and pump set up, and they started filling the truck first.

Meanwhile, Gunner made his usual investigation of the surrounding area, marking a few spots as he went.

The kids had things under control, so Ben headed around to the front of the truck. He laid the AR across the hood and leaned against the bumper. As he drank from his water bottle, he sized up an old motel across the street.

He wondered about the possibilities of spending the night in a motel at some point. There wouldn't be any supplies left in a place like that now and no reason for people to hang around. If they found the right place, maybe, but not this one. They needed someplace more remote. If they could park the truck out back or under some type of cover, it might work. It sure would be nice to sleep in a bed again.

He wasn't the young man he once was, and the sleeping bag and bedroll combo wasn't as comfortable as he remembered, at least not this many nights in a row. Sleeping on the ground every night and driving all day was beginning to take its toll on his back.

He never seemed to get enough rest, and no matter how tired he felt, he couldn't seem to sleep through the night. He wondered how the kids were doing but figured they probably wouldn't mind a real bed for a change, either.

Originally, Ben was going to let Joel finish the day out driving, but after that last little stunt he pulled back at the exit, Ben was having second thoughts. He was sure Joel hadn't done it on purpose, and that's what scared Ben the most.

They couldn't afford to get sidetracked with an accident out here in the middle of nowhere. They might not recover from a mistake like that. Then again, he couldn't be too hard on the boy. It had been a long day for all of them.

Ben reconsidered and decided to let Joel finish the driving for the day. He didn't want to risk embarrassing him in front of Allie by taking that responsibility away. And if he knew his son, Joel would be mindful of his driving from here forward out of the sheer desire to prove himself.

Ben could hear the kids talking as they switched from filling the truck's gas tank to filling the spare fuel cans. He walked around to the side of the Blazer where he could see them. Joel muscled the full jerry cans up onto the rear cargo rack and strapped them down. Meanwhile, Allie continued to turn the pump handle.

"Are you up to driving the rest of the way tonight?" Ben asked.

"Yeah, sure. What is it? Like another half an hour or so?" Joel rejoined Allie to help finish filling the truck.

"Probably not even that long. We're really close. I could use the time to study the map for tomorrow," Ben added.

"You both know I can drive, right?" Allie joked.

Ben looked at her and started nodding his head. "All right then. Maybe tomorrow. Let's see how the day goes."

· 19 ·

Once the truck was filled with fuel, Joel and Allie stowed the hose and pump and they all loaded up in the Blazer.

Ben stowed the AR in what had become its normal spot, between the passenger seat and the center console. The soft case that held the AR-15 remained in place and was loose enough to allow the short black rifle to easily slide in and out, more like a sheath or a holster. It was actually working out pretty well in that spot and made the gun available in a hurry, if need be.

Everything was starting to find a home in the truck through trial and error. They had been on the road for eight days now and it was beginning to feel like home.

Ben had always been a stickler for organization, and the four of them living out of the Blazer was no excuse to deviate from that practice.

He was particularly impressed that Allie had organized a small area in the back. She had brought a book to read and what looked like a small, well-used leather-bound journal.

She'd wedged them, along with her box of ammo and a few other personal items, between the seat and part of the wheel well. She had also constructed a spot for the sawed-off shotgun out of a rolled-up towel. The barrel pointed down and the pistol grip stuck up for easy retrieval from her side of the seat behind Joel.

The floor in front of Gunner was piled up level with the top of the rear bench seat on his side. It was mostly dehydrated food they hadn't even touched yet. Gunner had settled into his new seating assignment and had given up his attempts to occupy the front passenger seat.

Ben thought that had more to do with getting to sit with Allie than Gunner's good behavior. With the amount of attention Allie gave that dog, it was no wonder. Ben didn't mind, though. As far as he was concerned, Gunner could do anything he wanted. After all, he had most likely saved the kids' lives back in Kansas. And Ben had no doubt that Gunner would fight to his dying breath for that girl at this point.

They would definitely have to move some things around if they added another person. Of course, that was going to be the case sooner or later, regardless of Allie's dad joining them. They'd have to put some stuff on the roof. At least they had the other side of the roof rack open.

Ben now wished he hadn't talked Joel out of getting an old Suburban when he first started looking at trucks. That was originally what Joel had his heart set on, but Ben had convinced him otherwise.

He'd told Joel he thought it would be too big and long on the four-wheel-drive trails around Durango and that a shorter wheelbase Blazer was the way to go. Also, more importantly, he would need a second job to keep gas in a suburban.

That was one big advantage of the Blazer. Compared to a larger truck, the Blazer got decent mileage out of a tank, better than what Ben's conservative estimate had been. The whole routine of pumping fuel had become familiar at this point, and they had it down to a fairly efficient process.

The interstate remained littered with the occasional accident or abandoned vehicle to avoid, but they made good time and soon saw a sign for Vandalia, Illinois. According to the map, the Kaskaskia River was just beyond the town. The sign also listed Effingham, Terra Haute, and Indianapolis. Indianapolis was the farthest distance at 173 miles.

"If we get a good start tomorrow, we should be in Ohio by lunchtime or sooner," Ben said.

Of course, that depended on how long it took them to get around Indianapolis. Ben planned on giving the city a wide berth tomorrow. As tempting as it was to remain on the interstate, he knew better. They would stay on I-70 until just before Indianapolis, where they would head north, eventually picking up Route 30.

If they followed 30, it would more or less take them straight into Pittsburgh and allow them to miss a couple big cities in the process. Indianapolis and Columbus, Ohio, were the two big ones he wanted to steer clear of. After what they'd seen and heard, there was no second-guessing the decision to go around those areas. They had to make their way north eventually to get to Pittsburgh, so they might as well make it work to their advantage.

No point in bouncing back and forth between roads. They could get back on the interstate after Pittsburgh.

Ben knew if things went well they could get to the kids in Maryland within two or three days' time if they pushed it. For the first time since they started, he truly felt like they were making progress, and he was encouraged for a change.

"Here we are." Joel leaned forward in his seat and looked over the steering wheel at the empty shops that lined the streets. He slowed down a little as they passed through what was left of the town.

Ben was glad nobody was around. He didn't have the energy or the patience to deal with any more trouble today.

"No need to slow down," he reminded Joel, who seemed to be preoccupied with something out the side window. "Let's get to the river."

"Oh, sorry." He accelerated quickly, and they sped through without seeing so much as a single person.

The bridge was only a few miles outside of town and was two lanes wide on each side. The river itself was unremarkable and looked more like a giant ditch. It sat a good 50 feet below the interstate, so the bridge stayed at the same height as the road where it crossed. It was about 100 yards across the greenish-brown water.

Ben watched the slow current carry a stick downstream as they crossed.

"It's a little cleaner than the Mississippi. Maybe even fishable," Joel noted.

"It's worth a try," Ben agreed.

Once across the small bridge, they entered an area that was divided up with orange construction barrels that reduced the eastbound lanes into one single lane that funneled onto the westbound side of the road. They were in the middle of repairing a section of road, by the looks of it, and there was a break in the guardrail.

"How about down there?" Ben pointed to an opening in the barrels that led off the side of the road and back toward the river.

"Okay." Joel slowed down and made his way through the maze of construction barrels.

The grassy shoulder dropped off steeply toward the river, and they followed it down alongside the bridge until it reached the water's edge.

There was a clearing under the bridge in the shade and out of sight from the road above. Ben decided this would be a good spot, as the surrounding forest was too thick to navigate with the Blazer.

From here, they'd have a better chance of hearing someone coming on the bridge overhead, and after their last experience, he wanted to keep an eye on things tonight.

"Here?" Joel asked.

"How about under the bridge, over there?" Ben nodded at a place between two concrete support columns. The truck fit between the bridge supports with room to spare on either side.

Joel moved the Blazer to the spot, put it in park, and shut it down. They all unloaded quickly and gravitated to the water's edge to stretch their legs. Even though they had just been out of the truck not long ago, it somehow felt better this time.

Maybe it was the fact they all knew the driving was done for the day. Maybe it was the way the sunset was lighting up the evening sky. Whatever the reason, Ben felt the mood mimicked the relaxed rhythm of the lazy current. This would be a better spot than he had hoped to find tonight.

Gunner's loud lapping of water interrupted the still of the evening. Never one to let an opportunity go to waste, he then waded into the water and swam in a short little circle a few yards off the riverbank before returning to shake off and roll in the grass.

"Look at that. Do you see it?" Joel pointed to a ripple on the surface of the water. "There's another one." He pointed farther upstream.

Fish were rising to a fresh hatch of mayflies. Ben hadn't noticed the insects at first but now he could see them skating across the water by the hundreds in their death throes. Some type of fish was taking the opportunity to gorge itself on the spent mayflies as they gathered in groups on the surface.

Ben grinned at Joel. "Well, what are you waiting for?"

· 20 ·

Joel ran back to the truck without saying a word and returned a few minutes later with his fly rod and a small box of flies. He carefully selected a fly out of the box and held it up. "What do you think?"

"Looks like a good match." Ben noticed Joel had selected a dark-colored elk hair caddis. That's what he would have gone for, too. It was a close match to the mayflies.

Joel stuffed the fly box into his pocket and tied on the caddis fly before he waded out into the water a few feet.

Ben and Allie stood on the bank, watching as Joel began to cast to the rising fish.

"Gunner, stay," Allie said firmly, trying to keep Gunner from joining Joel.

The dog stood next to her, wagging his tail and whining as Joel waded farther out into the river.

"You'll scare all the fish." She held on to Gunner's collar as he leaned toward the river.

It wasn't long before Joel had a bite and brought the fish into his hand. He scooped it up by its mouth and unhooked the fly before turning to face Ben and Allie.

"It's pretty big, but I have no idea what it is." Joel grinned, holding the fish out for them to see.

"Maybe some type of carp. I really don't know, either, but it is a nice size," Ben said.

Allie laughed. "Well, don't look at me."

"Oh, wait," Joel said. "I know what kind it is. The kind that will go nicely with beans and rice." He laughed as he tucked his fly rod under his arm and pulled out his pocket knife. He quickly dispatched the fish using the knife and then threw it up onto the bank. "I'll see if I can catch a couple more."

When Gunner saw the fish land on the muddy bank, Allie could no longer control him and he broke free from her grasp.

"Hey, you!" Allie blurted out, but it was no use. Gunner was determined to investigate the new weird, slimy thing on the bank.

Ben snorted. "I guess that leaves me with fire duty. I'll get it started." He turned to walk back toward the truck.

"I'll help you unpack," Allie offered.

"Good," Ben said. "I've been wanting to talk to you about something."

"Oh, okay." She joined him on his way to the truck.

"I've been doing a lot of thinking. I would like you and your dad to continue on with us to Maryland."

"Really?" She smiled.

"I mean, you don't have to, and I'm not trying to tell you what to do, but the city isn't the place to be right now. I'm sure I can speak for Joel as well on this, and we just wouldn't feel right leaving you there. We want you to stay with us, Allie." Ben looked her in the eye.

Allie was all smiles and began to tear up as she ran to Ben and hugged him. "Thank you."

They stood there for a few seconds before she let go and stepped back. "I don't want to be a burden on you guys. I'm afraid my dad and I will just slow you down. I mean, my dad... Well, let's just say he's not like you and Joel and—"

Ben cut her off. "It's okay. It'll be fine. You can't stay in Pittsburgh if it's anything like what we've been seeing in the more populated areas." He climbed up to the roof rack on the truck and handed Allie the sleeping bags and tents from the top cargo box.

"Do you think we'll find my dad?" Allie bit her lip.

Ben handed her the last sleeping bag and closed the lid on the cargo box. He was stalling while he tried to think of something to say that didn't sound like he was pandering to her, but he also didn't want to sound too bleak. As he climbed down from the truck, he decided to tell her the truth. "I don't know, Allie."

She broke eye contact with him and glanced down at the ground for a moment before looking back up and nodding. "I know."

"I can promise you this. We'll do our best to find your father. I give you my word on that. Now, let's get this fire going." Ben put his hand on Allie's upper back as he moved past her and grabbed the shovel out of the back of the Blazer.

"I know you will. You have no idea how much this means to me."

"Sure I do. I have a daughter, too, you know." Ben smiled at Allie before he crouched down and started digging.

By the time Ben had the fire pit ready, Joel was walking up to the truck with a makeshift stringer of fish. The four large fish were still dripping wet as they hung from the small branch he had run through their gills.

"Here you go. All cleaned and ready to cook," he said proudly.

"Great job, buddy. How about putting them on the tailgate for now while I get this fire started?"

"Sure thing."

"Wow, that was fast. Four fish already?" Allie asked.

"Well, you know, when you're as good as me…" Joel joked as he sauntered over and began setting up his tent.

"By the way, it looks like you're stuck with me after all," Allie teased.

"What do you mean?" Joel asked.

Allie didn't say anything, smiling as she unrolled her sleeping bag.

Joel turned to his dad. "What's going on?"

"I asked Allie to join us the rest of the way to Maryland. And her dad, of course," Ben added.

Joel smiled and looked back at Allie, then quickly put his head down and got busy setting up his tent.

Ben could tell he was trying not to let on how happy he was to hear the news.

When the kids were done getting their tents and gear squared away, Ben sent them to pick up firewood. He got his tent up in a couple of minutes and turned his attention to starting a pot of water on the little gas stove.

The kids returned shortly, each with a good-sized pile of wood in their arms. Gunner was out in front, carrying a stick of his own as they walked back into the campsite.

Ben shook his head. "I see Gunner is helping out tonight."

"I don't think he's going to give that one up," Joel said.

Joel and Allie unloaded their piles of wood and twigs by the fire pit while Gunner found a spot nearby and lay down. He immediately began to chew the bark off the stick while holding it between his paws.

Ben got a small fire going in no time and spread the fish out on a small round metal grill across the top of the pit. If they were carp or some other type of bony fish. Their best bet would be to pick the meat off after they were cooked and mix it in with the beans and rice.

The fish cooked rapidly over the open flame and were done in no time. The white flakey meat separated from the bone easily and nearly filled the pot of beans and rice the rest of the way to the top. He added in some dry seasoning from the bag of things Allie gathered from his kitchen and stirred it all together. That would help the flavor a bit.

Tired of eating out of the pouches that the dehydrated food came in, he grabbed a few plastic plates from the truck. He'd used these for times when he had all the kids and they went car camping back home. Using the plates now felt like an extravagant luxury and it was a nice change from eating out of a plastic bag.

"Oh, fancy tonight, huh?" Joel said as he and Allie returned from the river, where they were refilling water bottles.

"Yeah, I thought it would be a nice change. We'll have to wash them, but I couldn't deal with another dinner out of a bag. Besides, this looks pretty good. It would be shame not to enjoy it." Ben held up a spoon full of the bean, rice, and fish mixture.

"It smells really good," Allie said. She unrolled Gunner's collapsible bowl and scooped a few handfuls of dry food into it. Gunner was already waiting at her feet as she worked.

He had abandoned the stick-chewing as soon as he'd seen the orange canvas bowl come out.

"Let's eat." Ben dished out three equal portions and passed out the plates. They dug in with fervor and there was silence around the little fire pit for several minutes.

Gunner finished what was in his bowl and patiently waited for leftovers. He sat near the fire, licking his lips and watching them intently. Ben and Joel finished theirs completely, but Allie had a few spoonfuls left over, which she gave to Gunner.

After dinner, they all chipped in and got things cleaned up down by the water. Ben and Joel headed back to the truck to give Allie some privacy. She wanted to freshen up and change her clothes.

"Come on, Gunner. Allie can't get washed up with you stirring up the water," Joel stated.

Gunner reluctantly exited the water, where he had been wading along the bank and stirring up the muddy bottom.

Allie nodded at Joel and mouthed the words "thank you" as he and Ben walked away. Gunner slowly followed a few feet behind them.

"Thanks," Joel said softly.

"For what?" Ben asked.

"For letting Allie and her dad travel with us. I know it's a lot to take on."

"We'll make it work. It might get a little tight, but we'll move some things around."

"What are we going to do when we get to Maryland? There's going to be too many of us to fit in the Blazer."

"I know. I thought about that. We're going to have to figure something out. Maybe we'll find another vehicle, or I was even thinking a small camper. The Blazer could tow one without too much trouble."

Joel nodded. "Yeah, that could work. It's not like we're going super fast on the roads anyway. That's a good idea." He paused for a moment and had a look on his face like he was about to ask something, but he changed his mind.

"What?" Ben asked.

"What's the plan when we get to Maryland? Do you think Mom will come back to Colorado with us? What if she doesn't want to leave and won't let Bradley or Emma come with us?"

"I'm thinking your mom will see things a little differently now, in light of what's going on in the world." Ben hoped she would, anyway. "We need to put our differences aside and focus on survival, and I'm hoping she agrees."

Suddenly, a sharp scream shattered the quiet.

"HELP!"

Allie was in trouble.

· 21 ·

"Allie, we're coming," Joel yelled.

He and Ben took off running toward the river with Gunner way ahead of them. Ben could hear Gunner barking and growling before they got there. Then he heard a snarl he didn't recognize as he pulled his Glock out and came down the riverbank.

He couldn't believe what he saw in the light of Allie's headlamp.

Gunner had his hackles up and locked in a standoff with what looked like a large gray wolf.

The wolf was several feet away and flashing its teeth with an intensity that sent chills up Ben's spine. Allie was backed up against a large dead tree that stuck out into the water and cut off her escape route. The .38 pistol in her hand shook as she held it out in front of her.

Gunner had put himself directly between her and the wolf.

"It came up behind me!" Her voice trembled. Ben was glad she hadn't taken a shot with Gunner in the way.

"Everybody stay calm! Gunner, heal up. Gunner, heal up *now!*" Ben's commands went without so much as a look from the dog, and if anything, he doubled down on his intensity.

"Is...is that a wolf?" Joel muttered. "It's way too big to be a coyote."

"Yes, it is," Ben answered.

The wolf was taller than Gunner by a few inches but much leaner. Its slender legs, designed for traveling great distances, led down to massive mud-encrusted paws. Ben couldn't help but appreciate what a magnificent animal it was. The last thing he wanted to do was kill it, but this wouldn't end well if he didn't step in soon.

As he raised his pistol, the standoff escalated and the two animals began to circle one another. The distance between Gunner and the wolf quickly shrunk to just a couple feet. Ben didn't have a clear shot without risking a ricocheted bullet at this range. He didn't want to risk hitting Gunner or, worse, one of the kids.

Gunner refused to back off in spite of Ben and Joel's repeated attempts to call him off. The tension continued to build until Gunner finally snapped and tore into the wolf with a fury that Ben had never seen the likes of before now.

"Gunner, no!" Joel yelled.

Allie screamed again as the two canines locked up in a whirlwind of hair and teeth. Ben could hear the snapping jaws as they struggled to latch on to each other. They rolled around, flinging dirt and pebbles in all directions and snarling in between attempted bites.

Ben felt helpless, and for the first time in a while, he wasn't sure what to do. There was no way he could take a shot while they were going at each other like this.

Then, out of nowhere, Joel came running down the bank with an unwieldy tree branch.

Ben hadn't even noticed he was gone.

The branch was at least 10 feet long and looked heavy from the way he was running with it. The end of the branch had a few smaller limbs sticking off and some of them dragged on the ground as he ran.

Joel plunged the end of the branch into the mass of fur and chaos. The two beasts separated for the first time since the fight had started. But by the looks of it, they weren't planning on staying that way.

The wolf backed off several feet and was beginning to circle around Gunner for another go. This gave Ben a small window of opportunity. He thought about firing a shot into the air in an attempt to scare the wolf away, but he felt that it would take more than that now that the wolf had drawn blood. Besides, he didn't want to have to worry about it coming back later. Ben took the shot. At less than 10 yards away, the 9-mm round to the wolf's vitals dropped it on the spot with little more than a yelp.

Joel and Allie ran to Gunner, who was still standing—but barely. The poor dog was teetering as he tried to maintain his balance on three legs. He held his right front leg slightly bent, just enough to take the weight off it.

"He's bleeding," Allie cried out.

Gunner slid to the ground slowly as Allie dropped down beside him. "Joel, get me that washcloth over there, but get it wet first," she commanded.

Joel grabbed the washcloth from a rock where Allie had earlier set her things to wash up. He dunked it in the river and wrung it out before handing it to her.

Ben started for the truck. "Don't let him move. I'll get the first-aid kit." He only made it a couple feet before stopping and spinning around to look at Joel. "Stay alert. There could be more."

Joel nodded and pulled out his gun. "Got it."

Allie had the washcloth wrapped around Gunner's leg when Ben returned and was applying pressure to the wound. She had his big brown head in her lap and was rubbing his ear with her free hand. Joel was still standing over them with his gun drawn.

"He lost a little bit of blood, but it's not bleeding anymore. Looks like a couple puncture wounds. He keeps trying to move his leg out of the washcloth, so I don't think it's broken." Allie tried to soothe Gunner as he lifted his head on Ben's approach.

"Let me take a look." Ben knelt and focused his headlamp on Gunners leg. Allie removed the washcloth, revealing three small holes in the outside of the leg, just above the paw. They weren't as bad as Ben was expecting based on the amount of blood. Gunner tried to pull his leg away as Ben inspected the wounds.

"Easy, Gunner. Easy there. Looks like he got you pretty good, boy." Ben rubbed Gunner's head as he checked him over for any more injuries. "Looks like that's it, thankfully. He'll be okay. We just need to get this cleaned up and wrap it so it stays that way."

Ben glanced up at Joel. "Did you see or hear anything else while I was gone?"

"No. Nothing. I think it was alone." Joel shook his head. "I didn't know there were wolves in Illinois."

Ben started pulling supplies out of the first-aid kit. "It's rare, but I've read about them migrating down from Wisconsin. They've made a bit of a comeback in the last few years."

"Apparently, they're not that rare." Joel stared at the dead wolf several yards away.

"Allie, I'm going to need you to keep Gunner still while I do this. I have to clean out the bite, and he's not going to like it."

"Okay, I've got him." Allie leaned down, putting her head to Gunner's as she stroked his neck and whispered sweet things to him.

Ben started by pouring some of the filtered water over the wound. Gunner tried to lift his head, but Allie coaxed him into lying back down and holding still.

"Okay, now get ready. He's going to feel this." Ben gently drizzled a small amount of hydrogen peroxide into the punctures.

Gunner squirmed, forcing Allie to throw her leg over him to keep him in place. "Easy. It's okay. Good boy. It's okay."

Gunner grunted and flashed his teeth in protest but eventually resigned himself to his treatment and settled down. His resistance eventually simmered down to only the occasional sad whine.

Allie took a deep breath. "I was just getting ready to wash up when I felt something behind me. I can't explain it, but I felt like someone was watching me. When I turned around there was a wolf staring at me, and he was getting closer. The wolf started to growl, and I screamed. Before I knew it, Gunner came flying down the riverbank and put himself between us."

Allie hugged Gunner tightly around the neck as she lay next to him on the ground. "You saved me again!"

"He's a good dog." Ben ripped open a small white packet of antiseptic gel and applied it liberally to the bite area. Next, he wrapped the leg in gauze from above the paw and all the way to Gunner's elbow. He ripped off a few strips of duct tape and secured both ends of the wrap to itself, then ran a strip around the middle. He smoothed it out with his hands as he looked it over.

"There we go. That should keep it clean. No more swimming for you, at least not for a little while." Ben rubbed Gunner on the head as Allie released her grip on the poor dog.

"We need to keep an eye on it and change the bandage out daily," he said. "The main thing is keeping it clean."

"I'm happy to help," Allie said.

Gunner got up on his elbows and let out a sneeze as he shook his head. Clearly glad not to be pinned down any longer, he gingerly sat up on his haunches, careful to use the injured leg sparingly. He sat there, panting, as he glanced around at the three of them and acted as if nothing had happened.

"Yeah, he's going to be fine," Joel said.

Ben didn't want to leave the dead wolf lying on the bank for fear it might attract more of them if there were any around.

"Give me a hand, will you?" he asked Joel. "Grab the legs."

Joel and his dad carried the wolf to the edge of the water and counted to three before they heaved the body as far as they could. Ben grabbed the long tree limb that Joel used to break up the fight and pushed the wolf farther out from shore and into a stronger current. They all watched as the lifeless raft of fur drift beyond the capacity of their headlamps. Even Gunner made the effort and limped over to watch the body disappear downstream.

"I think I'll wait until morning to get cleaned up," Allie said as she gathered her things from the rock.

"I don't blame you. Probably not a bad idea." Ben put the first-aid kit back together and they headed back toward camp. Gunner kept pace with them as he hobbled along, his right paw held limp and only lightly touching down between strides.

"At least he's using it." Joel nodded at the dog.

"Yeah. That's a good sign," Ben agreed as he watched Gunner struggle up the modest incline of the riverbank.

Gunner was lucky he hadn't fared much worse. They all were. Ben was almost certain there were more wolves out there. Wolves were pack animals and it only made sense there would more lurking in the woods. They were probably watching them now.

He'd only seen one other wolf in the wild, and that was on a backpacking trip to Glacier National Park in Montana.

The wolf in Montana had crossed the trail they were hiking and only paused long enough for Ben to get a glimpse of it. It was a dark-colored animal, unlike the one that snuck up on Allie. But the Montana wolf was scared of them. It tucked its tail and ran away after they surprised it on the trail.

The wolf tonight was aggressive and showed no signs of backing down. Why was that?

Ben was worried enough that by the time they got back to camp he decided to make an exception and build a bigger, more traditional fire. As they added wood to the fire, Ben dug out the main hole a little more to accommodate larger sticks and logs.

Just when Ben was starting to feel like maybe he was overreacting, a high-pitched howl that made his skin crawl interrupted the silence. The sound was unsettling, even to Gunner, who got up from his spot by Allie's tent and slowly moved closer to the fire.

They all looked at each other as the eerie melody trailed off into the tall pines just beyond camp.

"That was close," Joel said.

Ben nodded. "Too close."

· 22 ·

That settled it for Ben, confirming his fears, and he knew what they had to do. They would have to stay vigilant all night.

"Somebody's going to have to stay awake and keep the fire going. I'll take the first watch," Ben stated.

"No way! You've done too much today already, Dad. I got this." Joel had a serious look on his face, and Ben didn't have the energy to argue.

"All right then, you've got the first watch. But first, let's gather up as much wood as we can." Ben sighed as he realized his hopes for a good night's sleep were quickly fading. So much for recharging the battery and hitting it fresh in the morning.

"I'll stay up with you, Joel. There's no way I can fall asleep right now," Allie said as they began to scavenge for wood.

They scoured the perimeter of camp, careful not to stray too far outside the flickering light of the campfire as they gathered anything they could burn. They came up with a good-sized pile of wood, and Ben felt confident it would be enough to keep the fire going until morning.

"I think that's good." Ben stood back and eyed the pile of sticks and branches. Some of it was still green and was going to put off a fair amount of smoke—something he wasn't crazy about. But what choice did they have?

For an added measure of security, they all pulled their tents a little closer to the flames, forming a small circle around the now blazing fire.

"Not too close. We don't want any sparks to leap out and burn holes in the tents," Ben warned the kids. "As long as the fire is going, they won't come in very close."

But Ben wondered how true that was after the aggressive actions he'd just witnessed. He hoped that was an isolated case and the other pack members would be more restrained. One thing was for sure, though: the animals they had encountered so far were just as unraveled as the people they had run into.

It was almost like the animals could sense this was a time of weakness for them and were reclaiming the land from people while it was ripe for the taking.

Why had the coyotes and the wolf been so overly aggressive? He wasn't 100 percent sure about the wolf, but he knew coyotes didn't behave like that normally. Then there were those vultures attacking their tires the other day. What was all that about?

Ben shook his head when he realized how crazy he was sounding to himself. He needed to get some sleep. He wasn't even thinking straight anymore. "All right, guys. I'm going to try and get some rest. Wake me up in a few hours or when you get tired and I'll take over."

"Good night. I got it for a while. Don't worry," Joel said.

"Good job today! Thank you, again." Allie glanced at Ben and then back at the fire. "Night."

Ben smiled. "I couldn't do this without you guys."

He left Joel and Allie to the fire and Gunner to his stick. Ben thought Gunner looked remarkably well for just having tussled with a wolf and was glad to see the dog preoccupied with something other than his wounds. They also hadn't heard any more howling, which might be why Gunner had finally settled down, enough at least to resume turning his stick into splinters while he basked in the heat of the fire.

Ben tucked under the flap into his tent and slipped off his boots before pulling his feet inside. He rubbed his feet for a minute. It felt so good to be out of his hiking boots. They were great for hiking and had a lot of extra support, but they weren't so good for driving. And after spending all day in the rigid boots, they felt like two bricks on his feet.

He pulled the gun and holster from his belt next and tucked it neatly by the door near his head. He let the tent flap fall closed but decided not to zip it in case he had to make a quick exit. Allie and Joel were talking quietly, and every once in a while, he heard Gunner crunching on his stick. But none of that kept him from falling asleep in a matter a seconds.

Allie poked at the fire with a long stick. "Do you think the wolves will come back tonight?"

"I don't think so. At least I hope not. I mean, you would think they wouldn't try anything after what happened to the last one, but what do I know." Joel focused on sharpening a long straight branch he had found when they were gathering firewood. He had been working on it for a while now.

"What are you making there? Looks like a spear," Allie said.

"I don't know. Just fooling around." Joel was satisfied with the tip now and put away his knife. He thrust the tip of his spear into the red-hot embers at the base of the fire for a few seconds before pulling it out.

"And now you're burning it up?" Allie made a face.

"No. This makes it stronger. The heat takes the moisture out of the wood and tightens the fibers. See the carbon from the embers on the tip? And if you rub it on a rock you can get a smooth, sharp tip that's a lot more durable."

Allie laughed.

"What?" Joel said.

"How do you know this stuff? Your dad, I guess, right? Stupid question." She shook her head.

Joel shrugged. "I've been doing that since I was a little kid. Just something I picked up. We were always outside doing stuff when I was little. Both of my parents were big on sending us outside to play."

"Well, you're lucky." She smiled. "I've always lived in an apartment in the city. At least until my mom and I moved to Durango."

Joel noticed Allie's mood change as she let her hair fall over her face. She looked pretty in the firelight, but he wished she didn't feel sad. He slid across the last few inches between them and put his arm around her shoulder. She leaned into him, and they sat there without saying a word for a long time.

He stared into the fire as he pondered what type of future he and Allie could possibly have together in this new world. What was in store for any of them after Maryland? It wasn't like they could all go back to Durango and live happily ever after. No. The world had changed forever.

And they were changing with it.

For the first time, Joel didn't feel like a high school student anymore. He didn't feel like a kid anymore, for that matter. Something had awakened inside of him.

Maybe it was because he was thinking about the future for a change, or maybe it was the realization he would play a large part in determining if they survived or not.

· 23 ·

When Ben heard the song of a distant bird, he realized he had slept straight through the night. He rubbed his eyes as he tried to read the small numbers on his watch: 5:45. He could hear the forest coming alive with sounds outside the tent.

His first thought was that Joel had fallen asleep and failed to wake him for his fire watch. But when he smelled coffee and heard the kids talking, he knew that wasn't the case.

Throwing back the flap on his tent, he saw a smaller fire still going and a pot of coffee percolating on top of the metal grate. Joel had propped it up with a few rocks and positioned it over the now-larger fire pit.

Ben pulled his shoes on and slowly got up and out of the tent. "I thought you were going to wake me up?"

"Good morning," Allie said.

"Morning," Ben replied.

"I thought you could use the sleep. Besides, I wasn't that tired." Joel finished stuffing a few things into his backpack. "I didn't hear or see any more wolves after you went to bed, by the way."

"Good. I see you guys have been busy. Did you get any sleep, Allie?" Ben glanced around camp. Both their tents and sleeping bags were piled up by the truck and ready to stow in the cargo box. The only thing they hadn't packed yet was their personal bags.

"I did, but I woke up early for some reason." She shrugged.

Ben grabbed his coffee mug and poured himself a cup of the hot, steaming liquid as he inhaled the aroma. That smell never got old. After he took a sip and savored it for a moment, he set the cup down and immediately got to work cleaning out his tent and breaking it down.

Gunner hobbled over to greet him and Ben inspected the wrapped leg.

"It was wet and dirty so I changed the bandage when I got up this morning," Allie said.

"Good job. How did it look?" Ben asked.

"Thanks. It looked okay. I used the rest of the packet of antiseptic gel."

"Good." Ben gave Gunner a few scratches behind his ear and got back to work organizing his gear.

Allie began to boil some water in a pot and pulled out a packet of oatmeal from the truck. Joel remained seated on a nearby log with the AR-15 leaned against the side of it. He sipped his coffee as he stared off into the distance.

"I guess you can get some sleep in the truck today, buddy. Maybe Allie can sit up front and help me navigate for a while this morning."

"Sure," Allie chirped.

Joel nodded in agreement but remained silent.

He wished Joel had gotten a little rest last night. The poor kid looked exhausted. But Ben couldn't complain about the extra sleep he'd gotten. He was still stiff and a little sore, but he felt rested and he knew the extra sleep was needed.

If he got tired of driving later he could let Allie have a turn for a bit. Why not? She was perfectly capable, and if the roads were decent, he didn't see why not.

"I'll drive until the first fuel stop. Then you can take over for a while if you feel up to it." Ben looked at Allie.

"Yeah, sure. I can do that," she answered.

Ben was impressed with both of them this morning, and it gave him a good feeling to know they were putting so much effort into keeping things moving. These were good kids. Really good. They gave him hope for the future.

As the sun began to rise, the forest kicked into high gear. Birds and squirrels sprang into action with their calls and a flurry of activity and acrobatics from one tree to another.

Gunner did his best to keep track of the squirrels as they launched themselves through the air and scurried loudly through the branches. He ran from tree to tree as fast as he could with his bandaged leg while the squirrels raced up and down the tall pines, always just out of reach.

"Easy there, boy. You're going to hurt yourself," Joel warned.

It was just another morning for the woodland critters. But not for Ben and his crew. It would be a long day of driving if they were going to make it to Ohio by evening.

If they could get a solid eight or nine hours in, they might even make it to West Virginia or the Pennsylvania line. From there, it would be a short drive the next day to the outskirts of Pittsburgh and would leave them well rested for their rescue attempt. They'd need it if they were going to hide the truck and hike in.

"Do you think it would be okay if I went down to the river to clean up now?" Allie asked. "I have my gun, and I'll take Gunner with me."

"Go ahead. I'll finish breakfast. Just make sure he doesn't go in the water," Ben said.

Allie nodded. "Come on, boy. Let's go."

Gunner forgot all about the squirrels when he saw Allie walking toward the river. He chased after her.

"I guess the leg's feeling better?" Joel shook his head as he watched Gunner sprint after her.

"Yeah, I think he'll be just fine. Hey, Joel?"

"Yeah, Dad?"

"Thanks for letting me get some sleep last night. I really needed it." Ben climbed onto the Blazer and opened the lid on the rooftop carrier.

"I know. You did a lot yesterday." Joel handed the gear up to Ben as he stowed it away in the rooftop cargo box.

After they were done, Ben took the boiling water off the fire and added it to the oatmeal pouch. He folded the bag closed and set it on the tailgate to cook. By the time Allie returned from cleaning up, breakfast was ready.

"I feel so much better!" Allie pulled her hair back into a ponytail.

"I bet. I'll clean up when I take the dishes down after breakfast." Joel scooped a couple handfuls of dry dog food into Gunner's bowl.

He ran over and gave it a sniff but waited a while before eating. Once he realized that was all he was getting, he began to eat slowly.

Ben shook his head at the dog. "I'll help you with the dishes. I want to get cleaned up, too. Plus, we need a bucket of water to put this fire out." He divided up the oatmeal, and they all sat quietly as they ate their breakfasts and finished the last of the coffee.

Then he and Joel gathered up the dishes in the bucket and headed down to the river. Allie and

Gunner stayed back at camp while she packed her things into the Blazer.

Ben and Joel returned in a few short minutes and put out the fire before loading the rest of the stuff up.

Ben looked around at the campsite. "Well, I guess that's it."

"Come on, Gunner. Load up." Joel coaxed Gunner into the truck and then climbed into the back with him. Allie got in the passenger's seat and took the map out as soon as she was buckled in and had her window rolled down.

"Good idea." Ben rolled his window down, too, as soon as he got into the driver's seat. It was a pleasant morning and the air hadn't lost its coolness yet. It would be hot later and they should enjoy the cooler temperature while it lasted.

He started up the truck. The rumble of the Blazer's exhaust echoed under the bridge and cut through the quiet of the morning like a knife. Gunner was already lying down on his side of the bench seat in a tight ball as they emerged from the shadow of the bridge. The familiar tone of the Blazer returned as the echo faded behind them and they made their way back onto the interstate.

Ben stopped to look before pulling out, although he wasn't sure why. Old habit. There were no other cars in sight. It wasn't long before Gunner and Joel were both passed out in the back. Joel had actually fallen over on Gunner for a change and was using him for a pillow.

Allie looked back at them and smiled. "That didn't take long."

"I didn't think it would. You know, we're going to be on the interstate for a few hours before I need any help with the map. It's okay with me if you want to get a little rest, too. I know you didn't sleep well last night."

"Are you sure?"

"Yeah, go for it. I'm in good shape. You guys can take over later and give me a break."

"I won't argue with you. I am a little tired." Allie balled up her fleece and put it between her head and the doorframe. She was out within a few minutes, and Ben was alone with his thoughts.

He pondered a lot of things, but mostly his kids in Maryland and how he hoped they could hang in there for just a few more days.

· 24 ·

Both Joel and Allie slept long enough for the Blazer to burn through almost an entire tank of gas. Only Gunner got up at one point and pushed his head up alongside Ben's seat and out the window. He remained there for a few minutes with his face in the wind before he returned to his spot on the back seat with Joel.

Ben didn't need any help with directions right now, and there was no reason to wake Joel or Allie. He figured it was better that they get some rest so they could help later.

They were still using I-70 to make their way east, and there were the usual things to look out for on the road. But with the wide-open two-lane highway and generous grass median, it wasn't hard to spot an obstacle from a distance and easily avoid it.

Ben leaned over the wheel as he drove, scanning the horizon for any signs of a gas station. He glanced at the sky. Even though it was a clear day with very few clouds, it felt like the sunlight was being filtered through a yellow lens.

There was an overall haziness to the air, and Ben wondered if it was contributing to the heat index. The Blazer had air-conditioning but he was reluctant to use it and burn the additional fuel in the process. Maybe this was a normal temperature for this time of year in Illinois. It was the middle of June, after all.

Still, though, it felt unnaturally hot to him, and he wondered if the thick air was trapping heat in the lower atmosphere. The odd yellowish hue over everything was definitely a result of the EMPs. A mixture of dust and smoke, most likely, kicked up by the massive explosions.

He thought about the towering plume of smoke over St. Louis that had nearly choked them all. He could almost taste the debris particles in the air when they were at the first bridge.

How many times had that scenario played out all over the country? How many cities had been annihilated in the attacks? Pittsburgh would soon tell them a little more.

The changing landscape hadn't gone unnoticed by Ben, either. Had the kids noticed the change? They must have. They were too observant not to.

With each new day the agricultural fields they passed looked worse and worse. Ben had chalked some of this up to the fact that all the irrigation systems were down.

But now almost every field held dead or dying crops. Row after row of young corn plants withered away and dried out. Even the soil was beginning to crack and shrink as it formed a crust over the fields. If it was like this everywhere, the dead crops would only exaggerate the dire shortage of food.

The only things that seemed to be growing well were the weeds on the side of the road. The shoulders and medians were starting to show signs of neglect. There were no road crews to cut grass or do maintenance.

All of it added to the overall apocalyptic feeling.

It dawned on Ben that they hadn't seen rain since they left Colorado. He hadn't seen any rainclouds or storm systems moving through the plains, either. That was odd for this time of year.

The air was unusually dry, like all the moisture had been sucked out of it. The humidity level had to be extremely low. Ben found himself applying lip balm more often over the last few days to keep his lips from drying out and chapping. Had the nukes somehow affected the weather? Was that even possible?

He wiped a bead of sweat from his forehead and leaned slightly out of the open window. The air rushed over his face but provided little in the way of relief. Even at 60 miles per hour, the wind was hot and stale.

Gunner was sitting upright now and panting heavily, his big pink tongue hanging from his mouth. He leaned against the back of Ben's seat with his head propped on top of the headrest as he tried to take advantage of the airflow.

Ben felt bad for Gunner and reached his arm around the seat behind him. He searched the floor for Gunner's collapsible dog bowl. When he found it, he pulled it up and set it onto the center console.

Gunner sniffed at it right away.

"Hang on, boy." Ben kept one hand on the wheel and put a water bottle between his legs while he unscrewed the lid with his free hand. He emptied the remainder of the water into Gunner's bowl and barely got out of the way before the dog eagerly lapped it up.

"There you go. Feel better now?"

Gunner sat back on the seat when he finished. Ben shook his head as he glanced in the rearview mirror. Gunner was sitting over top of Joel now, with two long streams of water and saliva hanging from both sides of his mouth.

This was not going to end well.

"What... Hey! Gunner, move," Joel huffed as he sat up and wiped the drool from his arm. "Gross!"

"Sorry about that. He was thirsty," Ben said.

"Where are we?" Joel asked as he leaned forward between the seats, still squinting while his eyes adjusted to the glare. "It looks weird out."

"We just crossed the Indiana state line about 20 minutes ago. You guys have been out for a few hours."

"It didn't look like this when we left this morning."

"No, it didn't. I thought it would clear up when we got farther from St. Louis, but it's getting worse the more we drive east. It looks like mostly dust with a layer of smoke in the upper atmosphere. We could use a good rain to clear the air."

"It looks so dry." Joel took a drink from his water bottle.

Allie began to stir from her nap and she slowly sat up in her seat. "Where are we?"

"Indiana," Joel answered.

"What happened?" Allie rubber her eyes as she took in the landscape. "Why is it so hazy?"

"Yeah, we were just talking about that. Not sure what's causing it, though," Joel said.

Allie adjusted herself in the seat a little more and took a drink of her water.

"We're going to need gas soon, so keep a look out for a decent place, guys," Ben said. "After that, maybe one of you can drive for a while so I can figure out the best way to cut around Indianapolis and head north toward Pittsburgh."

"We're really getting that close?" Allie asked.

"Well, it's still a ways to go yet, but yeah, we're closing in fast," Ben added.

Allie managed a slight smile but didn't say anything more about it.

"There's a place." Joel pointed to the other side of the highway.

It was an average, run-of-the-mill interstate convenience store and gas station, and they would have to cross the weedy, overgrown median to get to it.

Ben slowed as they got close and turned into the median. Weeds brushed the underside of the truck as they crossed down and then back up onto the westbound lanes.

From there, they took the exit ramp and followed it into the gas station.

Ben drove the perimeter of the parking lot until he found the underground tanks. They were located close to the actual gas pumps, which meant he could park the Blazer in the shade of the roof that covered the pumping area.

They poured out of the truck without saying much.

"Stay!" Ben stopped Gunner from jumping out of the truck behind him. Scooping him up in his arms, he gently lowered him to the ground. Gunner hobbled off in search a suitable place to do his business. Ben knew Gunner should rest the leg, but it would be a while before they stopped again.

157

Heat radiated off the blacktop from the moment Ben got out of the truck. Even in the shade, the heat was brutal. Gunner made his way back over to the shade near the truck when he was finished and whined at Ben as he started to set up the pumping equipment. "It's too hot out here for you, boy."

Joel came to stand by his dad. "You want help?"

"No, I'll get the gas this time," Ben said. "But you could help Gunner back into the truck for me."

Joel nodded and opened the driver's side door. Gunner hopped up, put his front paws on the seat, and waited there until Joel boosted him the rest of the way up. Gunner made his way to the back seat and found his spot right away. Joel grabbed the AR-15 before he closed the door, and he and Allie walked around to the front of the Blazer while Ben got started pumping fuel. It didn't take long to work up a sweat, and Ben took a break after a few minutes to remove his sunglasses and wipe his face with his shirt.

Joel leaned around from the front. "Want me to finish up?"

"No. Almost done anyway. Just get ready to drive," Ben answered. By the time he had the tank topped off, he had worked up quite a thirst. He could put the hose and pump away in a minute, but right now he needed some water. He grabbed a fresh bottle from the back of the truck and gulped some down. It was far from cold, but it was wet.

He leaned against the truck and closed his eyes while he regained his composure from the heat.

"Hey, Dad?" Joel said.

"Yeah?" Ben responded without looking up.

"We've got company."

· 25 ·

Ben lifted his head quickly and screwed the lid back onto his water bottle. "Where?"

Joel and Allie were staring west down the interstate. Joel was using the scope on his rifle and had the magnifier in place.

Ben slid around the back of the truck and came up behind Joel.

"Here. Take a look." Joel handed the AR-15 to his dad. "There's a white truck back that way. It looks like it's just sitting there, watching us."

Ben saw it now, too. Maybe a tow truck, but it was hard to tell. The heat rising off the road distorted the image, making it hard to see details. He couldn't tell how many people there were—or if they had any weapons.

But they were clearly being watched by the white truck. Even more importantly, why?

"Allie, keep an eye on them. Joel, give me a hand getting the pump and hose put away." Ben left the rifle on the hood of the truck for Allie to use. "Use the scope and let me know if you see anything."

"Okay," Allie said.

Ben and Joel got to work stowing the hose and pump and were finished and ready to go in no time.

Joel ran back to the front of the truck, where Allie was balancing the rifle across the hood and still looking through the scope. "Anything new?"

"I think I saw a guy with binoculars looking at us. But the truck they're in… I can't really make it out very well. It looks odd."

Ben joined them on the hood, using his M24 and its more powerful 10 × 42 scope. "There are two people, and they are definitely watching us. I see the guy with the binoculars. The truck looks likes like an old tow truck maybe, but it looks like they've welded steel plating all around it."

The closer Ben studied their watchers, he could see that nearly the whole truck was modified with steel plate armor. A piece even covered the windshield and left only a long narrow slit in the middle so they could see to drive. The front bumper had been beefed up as well with two long pieces of steel that came out to a blunt point a few feet in front of the truck.

Even the wheel wells were covered with steel plating that hung over the tires and came to within an inch or two of the ground. The surface of the steel plating all looked to have jagged pieces of rebar welded in place at strategic locations. The truck was straight out of a Mad Max movie.

A gunfight with these guys wouldn't go well for Ben and the kids. From what he could tell, neither of the men standing by the truck was holding a weapon, but that didn't really mean anything. He was sure they had something with them in the truck. But he was also sure a gunfight wasn't their intention.

He wished now that he had saved a few pieces of that dynamite.

"That truck was built for running people off the road." Ben stood up from his hunched over position on the hood behind the M24.

Joel and Allie looked at each other and then back at Ben.

"What are we going to do?" Allie asked.

"We're going to have to outrun them," Ben said.

"Do you think we can?" Joel glanced at the strange truck.

"I think we have a good chance. All that steel plating is going to weigh them down."

"You don't think we should stand our ground and fight?" Joel asked.

Ben shook his head. "We won't be able to make a dent in that thing. It would be a waste of time and ammo. Outrunning them is our best bet. Come on, let's get in the truck. I'll drive." He grabbed the

M24 and slid it back in into its case before he tossed it in behind the driver's seat.

Joel and Allie ran around to the other side and loaded into the truck. Joel kept the AR-15 with him in the front seat while Allie got organized in the back with Gunner.

Ben started the Blazer and watched the needle on the fuel gauge rise to full. A good thing to see. As soon as he put the truck in gear and started inching forward, the white truck began to move.

"They're coming," Joel yelled.

"Hang on, guys!" Ben stomped on the gas pedal and the Blazer lurched forward, spitting sand and gravel from the rear wheels.

He took the same exit ramp they had used to come in from the interstate. It was the quickest way back to the open highway, where they would have the best chance of outrunning the modified machine. Unfortunately, using the ramp forced them to travel toward the other truck for a couple hundred yards.

As soon as it was possible, Ben cut sharply to the left, across the grass, and took a shortcut to the interstate. The tow truck had closed the gap significantly, however, and was gaining ground on them.

"They really moving fast." Allie's voice was filled with concern as she watched out the back window, which Ben had left open, thinking it would help cool down the truck.

He pushed the Blazer harder and the speedometer climbed to 70 and beyond. Looking in the rearview mirror, he could see the tow truck somehow still gaining on them. They probably modified the engine, too. It was the only way they could hit these speeds with all that steel.

"They're gaining on us," Allie shouted.

"What I wouldn't give for a stick of that dynamite now." Ben shook his head.

"Dad?" Joel said timidly as he produced an old towel from under his seat. As Joel carefully unrolled the towel in his lap, Ben caught a glimpse of yellow.

"Is that what I think it is, Joel Davis?" Ben looked back at the road and swerved to miss an abandoned car. The tires squealed as he forced the Blazer through the maneuver and wrestled with the steering wheel to straighten the truck out. Once he regained control, he glared at Joel.

"We gathered up the sticks you hid along the road at the bridge." He shrugged. "I thought you'd want them."

"You mean to tell me you've been sitting on 10 sticks of dynamite for the last day or so and didn't think to tell me about that?" Ben stared at his son.

"I know it sounds crazy, but I forgot. Please don't be mad."

Ben didn't know whether to yell at the boy or hug him. It was a stupid thing to do, but Joel might have just saved their hides. "You shouldn't have done that." Then Ben smiled. "But I'm glad you did."

· 26 ·

Joel grinned. "Cool."

Ben cut his eyes at his son. "We're still going to talk about it later. Right now, let's put that dynamite to good use. Allie, grab my small pack and look in there for the role of fuse."

"Okay," she answered as she started digging around.

Ben kept his eyes on the road. At over 80 miles per hour, one small miscalculation could end them. Thankfully, the road was clear for a good distance ahead. The only thing coming up was an overpass a few miles ahead, but the lanes were open underneath it.

"I found it!" Allie held the roll up between the seats.

"Good," Ben said "Now, cut off a piece about a foot long and give it to me when you get it cut. Joel, there's duct tape in the glove compartment. Start taping those sticks together in twos."

"Got it. Here, Allie." Joel handed Allie his pocket knife, then started taping sticks of dynamite together.

Allie went to work unraveling the stiff coil of fuse and cutting off a piece with Joel's knife.

"Here." She handed the foot-long length of fuse to Ben.

He took it. "There's a windproof lighter in the console. Get it out and light the end for me. We need to figure out the timing."

Joel nodded and flipped open the console. He found the lighter quickly, and as soon as he touched the jetted blue flame to the fuse, it erupted in a tiny shower of sparks. Instantly, the truck filled with a strong smell that reminded Ben of burnt gunpowder.

Ben switched the fuse to his other hand and held it a few inches out the window while he counted. When it had almost reached his thumb and forefinger, he let it go. That would do.

"Okay, cut five more just like that one," Ben said.

Allie grunted as she pulled the fuse against the knife blade. "This stuff is hard to cut."

"Here, let me help you." Joel worked with her until they had them all cut. Then he finished taping the sticks together in pairs. "Done."

"Gunner, easy boy. Down." Allie tried to calm down Gunner, who was now sitting up and leaning on her in an effort to keep the weight off his leg. All the activity and noise had gotten him worked up and he was trying to see what was going on.

Ben checked on their pursuers. Still gaining but not by as much. "Allie, take the fuses and attach them to the blasting caps sticking out of the end of the sticks. One fuse per pair."

Allie secured a section of fuse to each set of the bright yellow sticks like Ben asked. Then she laid them on the towel that Joel had put across the center console. "There you go."

"All right. Now, when I get the timing right, Joel and I will toss them out our windows. Allie, you man the lighter. I want to drop them all within a few seconds of each other. Okay?"

Both kids nodded in agreement.

Ben looked at Joel. "When you toss it out, throw it up in the air so it lands well behind us, just in case they go off on impact."

"Okay, got it."

Ben grabbed a bundle of dynamite and held it ready as he tried to estimate the distance he needed the tow truck behind him for this to work. There wasn't much time with the armored truck closing in fast. Any longer and it would be too close to use the dynamite.

Joel picked up a bundle and got ready.

Allie had the lighter in her hand and pressed the button a couple times, testing the flame. "I'm ready. Just say when."

They passed a road sign and Ben counted the seconds until the pursuers passed the same sign.

If he could time it right and create a string of explosions, one of them was bound to hit the tow truck or at least drive it off the road. Ben wanted to wait until they were under the overpass and use the shade to conceal the moment they threw the dynamite out of the truck.

His plan wouldn't work if the guys chasing them saw what they were up to and drove around the explosives. "Get ready to start lighting fuses when we hit the overpass."

Allie leaned up in between the seats and gripped the lighter firmly. "I'm ready."

Ben and Joel each sat poised with a bundle of dynamite in their hands as they waited for the right moment. Ben let off the gas pedal a little and the Blazer slowed as they drove into the shade of the underpass.

"Now!" Ben yelled.

Allie hit the button on the lighter and touched the flame to each fuse as they held them out for her.

Ben and Joel threw them out the windows and grabbed the next two bundles from the towel. She lit them right away and the truck filled with a flickering light as the shadows of the overpass blotted out the sun.

Joel grabbed the last two duct-taped sticks and held them up for Allie to light. As soon as the fuse started hissing, he stuck it out the window and heaved it up and over the truck like he had done with the others.

Before Joel could get his arm back in the window, Ben stomped on the gas pedal. His heart raced as they jolted out from under the overpass and back into the bright midday sun.

Ben glanced at the rearview mirror continually. The little yellow bundles of dynamite danced around on the asphalt before they came to a stop.

Ben counted down in his head as the tow truck sped toward the bridge. With any luck they wouldn't even see the explosives through the narrow slit of a window they had left themselves.

Joel and Allie watched through the back window when the first two bundles exploded.

BOOM... BOOM!

Both explosions were too early and missed the tow truck entirely. But they did cause the heavy ironclad vehicle to swerve erratically as the driver tried to avoid the shower of dirt and road fragments.

He must have seen the sparkling fuses in the shade of the overpass, but it was too late. With the extra weight welded on, the tow truck was unbalanced and struggled to maneuver at those speeds. The sudden turns caused it to lose control and slide as it leaned heavily from side to side.

When the next three bundles exploded in short progression, the blasts forced the truck off the road entirely. The dynamite might have missed it, but the concrete support column of the overpass didn't.

The tow truck plowed head-on into the massive round column at what must have been nearly 70 miles per hour. It hit so hard that the back end of the truck lifted up and kept moving forward while the cab folded like an accordion.

Two of the steel plates broke free from the body of the truck and were thrown past the concrete column. The whole truck shuddered from the impact before the back end settled on the ground once again.

"Did you see that," Joel exclaimed.

Ben nodded as he let the Blazer coast to a stop in the middle of the interstate. He got out and left the door open as he took a couple steps toward the tow truck to survey the wreckage. Joel and Allie stayed put in the Blazer. Ben didn't look for long. He got back in the truck and closed the door.

He thought about going back and putting them out of their misery if the crash hadn't done them in, but he'd changed his mind when he saw the severity of the wreckage.

Besides, if they had survived, they deserved the misery they were in. He was growing numb and had no compassion left for people that chose to live like this. Preying on others to survive was the lowest of the low in his opinion, and they deserved what they got.

Even so, he hated the callousness building up in him. He took a breath and tried to remind himself there were good people out there still.

There had to be. Or else surviving in this new world was going to be far worse than any of them could imagine.

· 27 ·

"So guess this is our life now, huh? Every day something crazy?" Joel shook his head.

"Yeah, but at least we're still safe and making progress. What other choice do we have?" Allie raised her voice.

"I'm just saying it's crazy. That's all. It's hard to believe what's happening sometimes." Joel shrugged.

Ben looked at the kids for a second. "It's probably going to get worse. I hate to say that but it's true. People are beyond desperate now and willing to do anything to survive, as you can see."

He turned to face out the windshield as he put the truck in gear and starting driving. "That's just the way it is, unfortunately, which is why we need to continue to stay alert and give no one the benefit of the doubt until they've proven otherwise."

Ben got up to speed quickly on the interstate, and before long, the overpass disappeared from the rearview mirror and their conversation.

"Do you want me to drive?" Allie asked.

"You know, I forgot all about that. I do, actually," Ben said. "I wanted to spend some time going over the map. I'll look for a place to pull off up ahead."

"I think Gunner has to go again. He's a little restless," Allie said.

Ben glanced in the rearview. "Maybe I can find somewhere to stop with a little shade."

They continued on for several miles until the next exit, where there was another overpass. Ben slowed the Blazer down but stayed on the interstate. He pulled under the overpass well inside the shaded area before parking off to the side of the road. He shut the truck off and they all got out. Gunner found a place to do his business before attempting to follow his nose after some distant smell.

"Come on, boy. This was just a quick one for you," Joel called.

Gunner hesitated and sniffed the air one more time before trotting back to the Blazer and jumping in on his own this time. Allie climbed behind the wheel and started to adjust the seat.

Ben looked at Joel. "How about taking the back again? If you pulled an all-nighter, you still need some rest. I need you 100 percent. I'll help Allie navigate. I'm going to have the map out anyway." Ben stepped aside while Joel hopped in the back with Gunner.

"Move over, dog," Joel said.

As soon as Ben got situated, Allie started the Blazer and pulled out onto the highway.

Allie kept both hands firmly on the wheel. "This is a lot different than my Jeep."

"Just be careful," Joel teased.

"Oh, don't worry. It's not like I'm going to sit on 10 sticks of dynamite for a couple hundred miles or anything like that," Allie shot back with a grin.

"Yeah, about that. How about letting me know important details like that from now on?" Ben laughed. What else could he do? There was no point in giving Joel too much grief over the dynamite now. There was a lot going on and he could forgive the forgetfulness. After all, it had saved them in the end.

"Sorry. But it all worked out, didn't it?" Joel sat back smugly in his seat as Allie sped up and got comfortable behind the wheel.

"It could have also gone very wrong," Ben warned. He was just glad they had escaped unharmed from their run-in with the tow truck.

He opened the atlas in his lap and began to study the route. "You're going to stay on this for a couple more hours, so just follow 70 for a while. I'll let you know when we get close to the turn."

"Sounds good. I got it." Allie brushed her hair out of her face, then quickly put her hand back on the wheel.

Ben thought she looked a little nervous, but she was doing fine and he was confident she could handle the Blazer. Eventually, the rhythm of the highway and the hum of the tires replaced their conversation as the miles rolled by.

Ben glanced back at Joel and saw he was close to falling asleep again. Ben was about to reach for his water bottle when he felt the truck shudder.

The Blazer hesitated and the smooth rumble of the engine was interrupted with short periods of sputtering that coincided with a loss of power.

"What's happening?" Allie looked at the gauges and then at Ben.

"I'm not sure. Give it gas again." Allie had been coasting since it happened, and he wondered if it was fuel-related.

She gave the Blazer gas, and within a few seconds, the truck shuddered again, repeating what it had done before.

Joel, fully awake now, sat up in the back. "What's going on?"

"It sounds like it's not getting fuel. Maybe the carburetor. Maybe the fuel pump. Look for a good place to stop, Allie." This was the last thing they needed but something that had been on Ben's mind since they left Durango, although he figured they'd most likely have problems with the truck overheating.

Pushing the Blazer while trying to escape the tow truck probably hadn't helped. Not that he'd had a choice in the matter. It was either that or God knows what at the hands of a couple highway bandits.

Ben sighed. They might have evaded the tow truck, but it had cost them. He just hoped it wasn't serious.

Allie headed for a shady spot under a half-wilted tree on the side of the road. She coasted under the tree and put the truck in park. Gunner sat up, panting and wagging his tail, blissfully unaware of the reason for the stop.

Ben hopped out. "Leave it running and stay in the driver's seat. I'm gonna want you to give it gas when I tell you. Can you pop the hood?"

Allie looked around as Joel leaned up and showed her where the hood release was before following his dad out and onto the road.

Ben unlatched the hood and propped it up. "Okay, go ahead. Just a little."

Joel stuck his head around the side of the open hood and motioned for Allie to give it gas.

Ben held his head close to the fuel pump and listened. It whined as she revved the engine. "Okay."

Joel relayed the message to Allie and she took her foot off the throttle.

Ben took the support out from under the hood and let it slam shut. He stood there for a minute as a bead of sweat rolled down his nose. He fought the urge to slam his fist down on the hood. They just couldn't catch a break. He had to keep it together for the kids' sake, though, and he let out a deep breath as he got his head together. "We have to find a place to hide the truck."

"We're going to leave it?" Joel stepped back.

Ben nodded. "After we get it hidden. We need to find a fuel pump."

"Can you fix it?" Allie asked.

"Yes. It can be fixed, but we need parts. We're going to have to walk."

Allie climbed in the back with Gunner and let Ben get back behind the wheel. Once Joel was in, Ben nursed the truck along the shoulder until he saw an opening in the woods. He steered the truck into the opening and headed away from the road.

Fortunately, the ground was bone dry, so it was easy going and they didn't need to engage the Blazer's four-wheel drive.

Ben stopped the truck after they had gone about 20 yards into the vegetation and turned the engine off.

He twisted to face the kids. "Well, let's get our supplies together and get the netting on the truck. Joel, bring the AR. Allie, I want you to bring your shotgun. It's five miles to the next exit. Maybe we'll get lucky and they'll have an auto parts store that hasn't been totally ransacked. Otherwise, keep your eyes open for any older Chevys on the road. We might be able to scavenge a pump."

The kids got to work loading up water bottles and anything else they thought they might need. Ben looked at the map once more for reference.

It wasn't the breakdown that really bothered him. They would deal with that. What weighed most heavily on his mind was the time this was adding to their trip.

He was worried about his kids in Maryland. How long could Emma and Bradley survive in this cruel, desperate world?

He hoped long enough. Because time was running out.

Find out about Bruno Miller's next book by signing up for his newsletter:
http://brunomillerauthor.com/sign-up/

No spam, no junk, just news (sales, freebies, and releases). Scouts honor.

Enjoy the book?
Help the series grow by telling a friend about it
and taking the time to leave a review.

ABOUT THE AUTHOR

BRUNO MILLER is the author of the Dark Road series. He's a military vet who likes to spend his downtime hanging out with his wife and kids, or getting in some range time. He believes in being prepared for any situation.

http://brunomillerauthor.com/

https://www.facebook.com/BrunoMillerAuthor/

Printed in Poland
by Amazon Fulfillment
Poland Sp. z o.o., Wrocław